*Armand*

# EMMANUEL BOVE
## *Armand*

*translated from the French
by Janet Louth*

THE MARLBORO PRESS/NORTHWESTERN
NORTHWESTERN UNIVERSITY PRESS
EVANSTON, ILLINOIS

The Marlboro Press/Northwestern
Northwestern University Press
Evanston, Illinois 60208-4210

Originally published in French in 1977. Copyright © 1977 by
Flammarion, Paris. English translation copyright © 1987 by Janet
Louth. Published in Great Britain 1987 by Carcanet Press Ltd,
Manchester. The Marlboro Press/Northwestern edition published 2000
by arrangement with Flammarion and Carcanet Press Ltd. All rights
reserved.

Printed in the United States of America

ISBN 0-8101-6056-0

Library of Congress Cataloging-in-Publication Data

Bove, Emmanuel, 1898–
    [Armand. English]
    Armand / Emmanuel Bove ; translated from the French by Janet Louth.
        p. cm.
    ISBN 0-8101-6056-0 (paper : alk. paper)
    I. Louth, Janet. II. Title.

PQ2603.O87 A8813 2000
843'.912—dc21                                           99-052866

The paper used in this publication meets the minimum requirements of
the American National Standard for Information Sciences—Permanence
of Paper for Printed Library Materials, ANSI Z39.48-1984.

*Armand*

1

It was midday. The cold made the sun seem smaller. The window-panes and shop-fronts did not reflect its rays. My attention was caught by anything that moved, as if I were a child. Occasionally I stroked a horse's head, on the forehead so that it would not bite me.

I was going along a street so narrow that the whips of passing carriages touched me, when a hand was laid on my shoulder.

I looked at it, then I turned round.

It was Lucien. Instead of calling out to me, he had played a trick on me by touching me in the street, as a stranger might have ventured to do.

I had not seen him for a year. He was wearing the same overcoat, a different tie, the same hat. He was neither fatter nor thinner. Nevertheless he had changed. As I remembered him he had no wrinkles, his skin was not chafed, nor was the dimple in his chin so deep that he could not shave it properly.

I stopped. Our breath was exhaled in the cold air but not in unison. I noticed a sort of sagging round his eyes which gave his face a sad and sickly look. The puckered skin there moved with the beating of his heart. Because his lower lip was thicker than his upper one, he seemed to be pouting. His nose was prominent, his ears, which I always hasten to look at, lest I should forget them, were brown and smooth, without the usual crease at the lobe, and so small that they looked as if they had stopped growing before the rest of his body.

Lucien had never worn a flower in the virgin button-hole of his overcoat. The lapels were misshapen. His hands in the torn pockets had nothing to support them.

We were embarrassed, Lucien for having greeted me so familiarly and I for appearing annoyed by it. We remained motionless. I waited for him to speak. Seeing him so poorly clad, the years of misery I had experienced passed before my eyes again. I had gradually forgotten them. Now they were as clear as if no interval separated me from them.

Smoke from the chimneys, like little clouds, obscured the sun from time to time. The canvas edgings of the blinds, lifted by the wind, lay on top instead of hanging free.

Finally we set off together. He put himself on my left, as if I were a woman, out of a vague respect for what is on the right. At each crossroads he was afraid I might change direction without warning. So I kept on saying: 'Straight on'.

It was still midday. Each of us looked to himself as we crossed the streets, without bothering about any possible accident to the other.

There was a café on the corner of a boulevard and a square which was smaller than it looked in photographs.

I invited Lucien to have a drink.

We sat outside where heating was provided by three silver braziers. We crushed pistachio-nuts under our feet. The siphons were enclosed in wire to stop them exploding.

Lucien took off his hat, put it down on a pedestal table, then, because he was always trying to guess what was considered proper behaviour, suddenly thought it was not the thing to put a hat on a table and picked it up again.

With a cigarette smoking at both ends between my

fingers, my neck protected by my turned-up collar, I looked at the passers-by. It was my father's way of amusing himself. Since his death, freed of the fear that he might surprise me copying him, I have applied myself, without much pleasure, to watching people coming and going and to finding some amusement in the difference of their faces.

Lucien had ordered a cup of coffee on which floated foam like that produced by saccharin. He was embarrassed. His fingers, which were all much the same length, twitched in a way which made the bones to which they were joined stick out right up to the wrist.

He turned towards me. He was eating a croissant, beginning with the point in the middle. Our eyes met. For a second I could see my head and shoulders in his pupils. I lowered my eyelids, without quite closing my eyes. They were drawn to his whole face. I realized that he was preparing to speak. The arch of his eyebrows became more pronounced. He opened his mouth, so slowly that his lips recovered their colour before they separated. I saw his tongue, short like his fingers, rise to make a sound. I was already listening. He made a gesture.

'How you have changed, Armand! You must be rich now. You could not come to our restaurant any more. Do you remember last year?'

The soda-water was still bubbling in my apéritif. I held my cigarette where it was dry to throw it away. I took a fresh one. It was so sunny I did not know if my match was alight or not.

Indeed I could remember my past life. That was finished now. But I guessed that Lucien himself still took his meals in the same restaurants and lived in the same room.

So that he should not reproach me for having changed, I tried to recover my former bashful and

9

uncouth manners. I was ashamed of my warm over-coat and especially of my silk tie. I pretended that I took no care of my clothes and when a drip fell on to my coat I let it make a stain.

Nevertheless it was useless for me to speak the same words, make the same gestures, I could not become what I had been before. The comfort in which I had been living for twelve months had brutally put an end to all my old habits. I could say more. It seemed to me that I no longer had anything against people. Those who complained seemed embittered or lacking in clear-sightedness because of their poverty.

Lucien looked at me without malice, but with an earnestness which, in an enclosed space, would have made me blush. I experienced that embarrassment which eyes too close to me caused when I was a child.

That day, ten years later, I became shy again for a moment. With an instinctive movement I turned away my head so that he should not see my ears, so that the parts of my body that I could not see even in a mirror should not be revealed to him too clearly.

I stayed like that for a few seconds. I even thought that I was going to blush. The blood rushed to my head, but too feebly to colour my cheeks. Now that I am thirty I often blush like that and I am the only one who knows it.

Then, glancing at Lucien again, I became aware that he was made of flesh, as I realize that I am when I look under my tongue in a mirror.

He was alive. His nostrils could recognize smells. On a day when several of them were mingled together he had been able to separate and count them. He did not make mistakes about the noises he heard. He could see the time from as far away as I could. He breathed at a rate scarcely slower than I did. The skin of his face went on below his collar. He had nipples, dark because he was olive skinned, hair on his chest, a navel closed or open depending on the midwife's skill.

I recovered my confidence. It was a man like myself who was watching me. The blemishes he found on my face I could have found on his.

A saucer fell from a nearby table without breaking. The blinds flapped noisily in the wind. Their brass supports slid up and down in dry grooves. Puffs of gas from the braziers surrounded us. Each time Lucien coughed drily as one does at the beginning of a cold.

With our legs parted by the single pedestal of the table we took care not to touch the underneath of the marble with our knees. From time to time I surprised him voicing some stupid opinion. I always agreed with him so that he should not think I had become proud. But I was aware that it was that very thing which betrayed me.

At one moment I felt like questioning him familiarly, calling him by a nick-name, as I had done in the past. I did not dare: he could not have endured it.

I scrutinized him furtively. He had drunk his coffee; with his glass at his mouth he was waiting for the undissolved sugar to slide down to his lips.

Then I remembered how he used to burst into laughter and get quite carried away. But now, beside me, he did not even venture to speak.

With my hand between my legs to pull my chair forward, I drew closer to him. He recoiled slightly.

'Are you afraid of me?'

'No, no, it was an instinctive movement.'

He fell silent. He was trying to control himself, as if he expected me to pretend to hit him for a joke. He had clenched his hands so that his fingers did not give him away by starting at some sound.

So much childish fear in a man moved me deeply.

'Lucien, come and have lunch with me tomorrow.

I'll say who you are. I'll try to find you a job. It will all come right. We shall be more comfortable than here. You will see my friend. She is very nice. We live at 47, rue de Vaugirard.'

'Is lunch at twelve?'

'Yes, come a bit later so everything is ready.'

A smile played round his lips. His blue eyes rested on me for longer than usual. He stammered out a few words. He showed a faint sign of pleasure.

It was half past twelve. The clocks were still striking. I called the waiter. He did not come. I had to look for a penknife in my pocket to make enough noise.

Lucien had got up. He was waiting until I was on my feet before he put on his hat. He had some crumbs of croissant in the turn-ups of his trousers. While I counted out my change he warmed himself at one of the braziers, with his overcoat open so that the heat could get to his body more quickly.

We took a few steps along the boulevard, indecisively, as if we did not know each other, and stopped beside a tree younger than the others which, beside us, seemed a bit like a third person.

'Well, Lucien, I'll leave you now. You know I'm expecting you tomorrow. Be sure to come.'

He did not reply. He lowered his eyes, which gave his face, because his eyelashes were all the same length, the look of a little girl. He had hoped for a lot more from our meeting. No doubt he did not know where to go. I thought of taking him home with me straight away, but I dared not, because it would have annoyed Jeanne.

I gave him my hand. He took it and held it as an old man holds the hand of a young benefactor, without a change in his expression, without putting one foot in front of the other.

12

'Are you going already, Armand?'

His eyes begged me to stay.

'Yes, Jeanne is waiting for me.'

He let go of my hand. I saw from his face that he would have liked to go with me, see me going into my house, wait until only a door separated us.

A few seconds passed. I still hesitated. I was expecting him to leave first. Patiently he waited for me to take a decision.

Again I gave him my hand, boldly, so that he should give me his, even if he did not wish to. He shook it. Joined like that the hands seemed to me for a moment like some sign. Then I left him pointedly, without turning round or speaking to him from a distance.

I went off nowhere in particular. In the straight streets, which had been quiet for an hour, the wind was blowing as strongly as it was above the houses. Although I was moving forward, the shadow of the street-lamps kept the same angle. On the horizon yesterday's clouds were crowded together as if, under other skies, other clouds were preventing them from passing.

2

The next day, when I made my way into the dining-room, Jeanne, hesitating over the knives, was laying the table.

The doors of the sideboard were open, revealing too many plates for the pair of us. The clock which does not work showed twelve o'clock in order to mislead as little as possible. The sun, which had lit up the room during the morning was moving away, as if the day was already at an end.

Jeanne had put some mimosa in a glass vase, although I do not like seeing the stalks, but she always chose it, whether for roses or for long-stemmed violets.

She was wearing a Japanese kimono which she found difficult to put on because she got the sleeves mixed up with the pockets.

She came up to me and kissed me several times. I saw myself against her body in a mirror. She thought I had closed my eyes. I had my arms round her waist. Her head rested on my shoulder.

Although Jeanne is as tall as I am, she always made herself behave as if she was not very tall.

'Jeanne, go and get dressed, he will be here soon.'

I was ready. I had put on a dark suit, a light waist-coat, a tie which Jeanne had made for me as well as she could, for she did not really know how to sew for a man, and some button boots which she had bought to make me look older.

As time passed, the freshness of my face, the shine of my hair and the creases of my clothes began to disappear. It is only immediately after I have finished dressing, for just a few minutes, that I feel completely as I should be. Then I speak with animation, my movements are easy. I am another man.

I should have been glad if Lucien had arrived at that moment and yet I was sorry I had invited him.

His bashfulness and over-familiarity would keep on reminding me of the man I had been. His table-manners would be bad. He would stammer when my friend spoke to him. He would take his bearings from me so obviously that it would look as if there were still links between us, as if he were here not out of kindness, but because of our friendship.

I was excited. Because I had nothing better to do and was nervous, I wandered from one room to the other. If our windows had not looked out on to the courtyard, I should have been watching for him. Sometimes I stopped in the hall, listening for someone coming upstairs, looking at the electric battery up on the wall, even though the wire did not vibrate when somebody rang.

Jeanne, helped by the daily woman, was getting the lunch ready. She was making as much effort as if we were expecting her brother, exerting herself not to forget details which Lucien would not notice.

I was afraid she would be sorry she had taken so much trouble when she saw him. To spare her disappointment I went up to her as she came into the dining-room carrying a pile of plates as maids do in comic pictures.

'You must not wear yourself out like this. My friend is a very simple chap. He has always been poor. I invited him mainly because I was sorry for him. . . .'

Jeanne was surprised. I had spoken so warmly of Lucien to her in order that she should not reproach me for inviting him, that she did not understand why I was

15

now voicing reservations. She was tender-hearted. She would rather believe good than evil. I realized that my words put her out, that for a second she suspected me of selfishness and jealousy.

However, I carried on:

'Pay no attention to his silences. He hardly ever speaks. He has never been part of a family. . . . He behaves very badly but he is very nice.'

I went out and sat down in the dining-room. The fifth time I went into that room I was delightfully surprised by the sight of the table-linen, the flowers and the branch of mandarin oranges on the sideboard.

I tried to read a paper, but only the biggest advertisement interested me. I swung my leg up and down impatiently. The movement soothed me a little, which made Jeanne think I suffered from a nervous illness every time she caught me at it. Sometimes, in a spasm which made me clench my teeth, I contracted my calf-muscles as if I wished they were bigger so I could show them off.

The minutes were going by. I lit a cigarette. To avoid smoking in the dining-room, I went into the drawing-room. A film of dust, already enough to write in, covered the furniture. I sat down once more, without crossing my legs because Lucien could not be much longer, and, with my hands together, twiddled my thumbs in opposite directions without pleasure, without realizing how much people poked fun at this trivial distraction.


There was a sudden knocking. It was Lucien. He did not ring.

I stood up. My chest was tight. Nevertheless I had no difficulty in breathing. The newspaper which I had meant to put on the chair had fallen on the floor. I felt a chill between my fingers.

I met Jeanne in the hall. I said to her:

'It's Lucien. Let me open it.'

My voice, because it is very close to my ears, seemed to tremble. It was as if it did not go all the way round, as if I heard it from inside. My hands were slippery with sweat as if I had been patting a horse. I did not know if I was flushed or pale. A cold draught passed over my face.

I turned the switch right round so that it could not go off by itself. The feeblest light-bulb in the flat lit up the hall. I trembled as I drew the bolt and gave myself a deep scratch on the nail of the door-handle.

It was Lucien. Standing on the door mat, he seemed taller. I noticed immediately that the hand he had knocked with was out of his pocket, that his hat was still on his head and he was looking past me into the flat.

We stood like that for a moment. I did not invite him in nor did he say anything. I was embarrassed at not wearing a hat or overcoat, at being home while he was still outside.

At last I stepped aside. He turned round because every time he left anywhere he was afraid of forgetting something, then he came in. For a moment our rôles seemed to be reversed, he lived in the flat, I was visiting him.

He stopped immediately. I pushed the door to from a little distance, casually, so that he should not suspect me of locking it. He was looking at a walking-stick I had found and dared not use. I put out my hand so he could give me his hat. He put it on the walking-stick, which, for a brief moment, looked as if it belonged to some reveller. I helped him to take off his coat. I hung it on the worst hook on the coat-stand as the others were full. Then both of us were bare-headed and coatless. I recovered my composure.

Lucien, with his hands stuck straight into the pockets of his buttoned-up jacket, turned towards me and, speaking low, assumed the air of an accomplice.

Although he was feeling very awkward, he was determined to appear at ease. He wore an expression aimed at making me understand that I was smarter than he, that I had been able to make the most of my chances. I pretended not to understand, because I was so afraid that Jeanne, opening a door without warning, might surprise us.

'Shall I go in?' he murmured, stretching up to my ear, his hands ready to press against the walls if he should lose his balance.

'Yes, of course. I'll show you the way.'

I preceded him into the dining-room. He followed me. I went up to the window. He still followed me. He wanted to keep near me.

So I saw him in full daylight.

The stripes of his trousers were broken at one knee by a tear which had been stitched up instead of being invisibly mended. He had put on a stiff collar and a black tie, one end of which must have been longer than the other under his waistcoat. His jacket, buttoned from top to bottom, was strained round him. For him, having his buttons done up was a necessary part of paying a visit.

He kept on looking all round without inhibition, as if he knew nothing belonged to me. Suddenly, he turned his gaze on me, then winked.

I had the feeling that this man would always live in poverty, that he was bound to it for ever because of his insolence to his benefactors.

However, I could not stop myself responding with a wink of the right eye, because I can only wink with my right eye, and it was very rapid, just like my sister's when she amuses herself by copying the street-girls.

Lucien was now standing by the sideboard. He was trying to see its upper shelves, between the open doors, without bending down. He was behaving as if I was not there. From the glances which he occasionally directed at the door, I realized that he was fearful only of Jeanne. He was even acting in a way that I understood. A feeling of self-esteem led him to make me understand that he had just as much right to be there as I, that it was only luck that made the difference between us.

I wanted to speak to him. I hunted for a subject about which he would be unable to say anything wounding.

'Sit down, Lucien, it will not be long till lunch.'

He went round the table and made for the fireplace.

'Sit down, Lucien.'

He looked at himself in the mirror, between the clock and a candlestick, then, since he could see the whole room reflected there without moving his head, he kept his eyes on it.

'Do sit down.'

He was on the point of obeying when the door opened. Jeanne appeared in a light-coloured dress, with bare neck and arms and a pendant necklace in the form of a hand. Although her ears were pierced, the earrings with which she had adorned herself were held in place by little screws. She was wearing lipstick and, like actresses, had drawn the top lip better than the bottom one. Her hands were empty. Because she had just finished washing, she was mechanically turning her wedding ring on her finger to dry it off.

Although there was only a feeble light in the dining-room, she seemed dazzled. She stopped as soon as she was through the door and turned her eyes to the window. It was as if she had just left off doing something important.

A moment later, as if she had only just seen us, she smiled.

I have often noticed Jeanne behaving in this way. She likes to seem surprised. She is tall. In order to emphasize her femininity she tries to appear absent-minded, artless and easily surprised.

She came forward. Having a visitor made her so happy she did not notice how shabbily Lucien was dressed. She wanted to put him at his ease at once and, as she walked towards him, she offered her hand from a distance.

I introduced my friend to her. He had clicked his heels in a reflexive movement, forgotten since he had been demobilized. His shyness vanished as he stood stiffly to attention. Only his hand in Jeanne's, as it were detached from the rest of him, betrayed him.

'Armand has told me a great deal about you,' said Jeanne, passing back and forth from the light-hearted to the serious with what she felt was elegant swiftness.

She looked at me in such a way as to show me that she knew how to get on with anybody. Like many women she thought that a significant look could only be understood by the man she loved. I was embarrassed. I realized that Lucien had guessed what the look meant.

He had blushed. Little drops of sweat stood out on his forehead. His shyness inhibited him. Jeanne over-awed him. He felt lost in that room. For the first time he gave me a look which overwhelmed me, so humble was he.

For a few seconds no one spoke. Lucien, his hands together, gazed at the vase of mimosa. The flowers, which, like him, had come from outside, were a comfort to him.

'Well, please come to the table.'

I sat down. The table had been laid so that the conventions were observed and yet I still had my usual place.

Lucien remained standing. He dared not touch a chair for fear of scratching the parquet.

'Lucien, we are going to have lunch.'

This time he sat down, looking under the table where things were complicated, before stretching out his legs.

Jeanne, between us, began to serve.

Although Lucien took care to copy all I did, he did not notice that, when my soup was finished, I left my spoon on my plate. He put his on the tablecloth.

At table, seated as I was, as everyone sits, in that dining-room, it would have been enough for him to speak, to make gestures, to become a man like any other.

Because the daily woman had stayed on, Jeanne had put a bell on the table. She rang. So little accustomed was she to doing this that at first she did not know how hard to press it, and, although she had put her finger on the button, no sound was produced.

There was silence as the daily woman changed the plates. Before putting them on the table she looked at them slantwise to see if they were shiny. She had put on a white apron. However, it did not make her look like a real maid.

'Well, Lucien?'

He raised his head. I was carving the chicken, lingering over the wing-joint, where I felt surer of what I was doing.

'How do you like the lunch?'

He hesitated for a moment, took in everything on the table with his gaze and at last said:

'Very much.'

'You are enjoying yourself?'

21

'Yes.'

'You must come here often.'


It was decided that we would have coffee in the drawing-room. I was trembling as I did after every meal. Jeanne folded up her table-napkin and mine. Only Lucien's remained unfolded on the table.

As there was no door from the dining-room into the drawing-room we had to go through the cold and dreary hall, past the kitchen where wisps of smoke floated.

A gas heater, made to look like a blazing log, burned in front of the drawing-room fireplace. The piano, the key of which was in the possession of the flat's owner, was locked. There was a pair of pictures, even though they were not the same size. There was a rug lying diagonally, as if it had been thrown on to the polished parquet. The curtains, held apart by cords, fell in a curve which Jeanne adjusted several times a day.

'Sit down, Lucien.'

He indicated several seats.

'Yes, there.'

He settled himself, having first inspected his chair carefully, as one does in a park.

The daily woman brought in the coffee and put the tray on a Chinese fretwork table which was scarcely higher than a footstool.

I cannot say whether Lucien at that moment re-membered that he had hardly said a word, or if he suddenly felt more sure of himself, or if he was struck by the appearance of the table to such a degree that he could not refrain from making a comment, or whether he wanted by a flash of wit to show himself in another light. At any rate, no sooner had the daily woman withdrawn, than he said in an ironical tone:

'That's not a particularly tall table, is it?'

I was sitting by the piano, on the stool which does not revolve, with my feet near the pedals. I looked at Jeanne. She shrugged her shoulders in the way I expected. I realized that she was offended.

She had bought that table so that the drawing-room, which was cold and unfriendly when she had rented the furnished flat, should look a bit cosier. She herself had made the blinds and the pouf on which she was sitting awkwardly. She called this flat her interior. She had wanted net curtains halfway up the windows, an electric lamp for the bedroom. She tried very hard, by moving certain objects about, even if it made us less comfortable, to give indications of a woman's presence. So Lucien's comment wounded her deeply.

'What do you mean, Lucien?'

The fireplace and the piano, both looking as if they were made of black marble, showed the same reflections in one place or another. The log, streaked like an arm of stone in an archway, had become rosy. The room was lit by the dim light from the courtyard.

He did not reply. He had realized that his remark had cast a chill. His face became expressionless, his elbows were pressed against his body.

Jeanne stood up. She brought him a cup of coffee.

He did not want to take it.

'What's the matter, Lucien? Take the cup, then.'

His features relaxed. He grabbed the cup so clumsily that Jeanne did not know exactly when to let go of it. Then, at first with small sips, then at a gulp, he drank his coffee.


Although it was still light outside, inside it was already getting dark. Jeanne had left the room. The daily woman had only a quarter of an hour left to do.

23

Lucien, sitting in an armchair, did not move. The log of the heater was still in one piece. The window-panes were slightly misted with steam.

We were not talking to each other. He had not stood up since we had come into the drawing-room. With his elbows on the arms of his chair, he kept on gazing round at everything.

'Perhaps it's time you were going home.'

He started. His mouth half-opened. Deprived of support, his lips trembled. He raised his eyebrows and frowned alternately without once closing his eyes.

There was so much distress in his look that I suddenly remembered how he was situated.

I stood up. He watched all my movements. I went up to him.

'Lucien!'

He clasped his hands as hard as he could, trying very hard not to let a gap appear between them. Then he stopped doing it. His hands separated. With his fingers still spread out without his being aware of it, he looked at me.

'You can't stay here. It's not my own house.'

He seemed not to hear. From time to time, as if there had been somebody there, he glanced at the elaborately carved table.

'Come along, then.'

I took his hand. Although it was bigger than mine, I wanted to pull him up as I did Jeanne when she was sitting on the grass.

He stiffened and gently freed himself.

'You don't mean it, Lucien. You must go home. I'll come and see you tomorrow afternoon.'

He listened carefully. His jaws trembled under the skin at the point where they joined.

'Will you really come?'

'I promise.'

Reassured, he stood up. I led him into the hall.

The drawing-room door was still half-open. We could see the log glowing. Its warmth followed us. Seen like that, from a distance, the room looked cosy in the half-darkness.

Suddenly, before I had time to stop him, he went back into the drawing-room.

'You must see that it's late, Lucien.'

He had sat down in the same armchair, had settled his elbows in the same way and had crossed his legs so that it would be difficult for me to pull him up.

'You must go, Lucien. I'll come and see you to-morrow.'

He did not want to go. He would have stayed there for ever. He was afraid of being alone.

I shut off the heater like the lights in a theatre. I opened the window, drew back the curtains, and took the cups into the kitchen, all in the same hand, so I could open the doors.

When I came back he got up, took a few steps and stopped.

'So I have got to go, Armand?'

'Yes, it will be getting dark.'

He came near me. I guessed he was on the verge of tears. Behind his pinched lips he was biting his tongue. He took my arm and squeezed it with all his might. He bowed his head. He was holding his overcoat so awkwardly that the pockets opened towards the floor. He stayed like that for a few seconds, leaning on my shoulder.

Then, comforted by some resolve, he went into the hall.

'Goodbye, Armand.'

On the landing he turned round and bent down to look behind me once more. He would have tried to go back into the flat if I had not blocked his way.

Now, facing the stairs, he was thinking.

I closed the door. I listened. I did not hear him going down. I opened it again. With his hat jammed on to his head so that he should not drop it, he was putting on his coat. He did not see me. I shut the door again silently.

3

About four o'clock in the afternoon, as I had promised, I went to see Lucien. Jeanne was at her brother's. She liked getting back late. I was free till dinner-time.

It was the same weather as the day before. Every morning for a week there had been in the blue sky the same streaks of white which vanished about midday. Every morning the sun, one minute earlier because the year had turned, appeared unobscured by a single cloud.

I walked quickly. I like visiting a friend, penetrating the secrets of a room, guessing what objects are for and the reasons why they are put where they are.

As I went along the streets became narrower, the houses lower, the crossroads less marked because the streets kept the same names on both sides of them.

In the cold, the lights which first came on in the hairdressers' and the shops of bric-à-brac dealers did not join up and had rays coming from them like the ones children draw.

Towards the end of that winter afternoon the sun was no higher than at sunrise. Because it was so feeble, I took the opportunity of looking at it. It had marks on it, like the moon. It was as if it had come back after having gone to bed.

Lucien lived in an old house whose façade was crumbling. It was tempting to scratch off the flakes, like the bark of a tree, to uncover the smooth fresh wall underneath. The staircase, like that in a monument, went up between two damp walls. An iron rail fixed on one of them served as a banister.

I went under an archway paved with dry cobble-stones. I crossed a courtyard which was used by several premises, one of which looked on to a different street. Some handcarts were stored in one building. I passed in front of the open door of a cellar where the flame of a candle disappeared without anyone protesting. I entered a corridor which the tenants went along counting their steps or even with their eyes closed, it was so dark.

The cold made me so sensitive that I took great care not to bump myself. Before I had got used to the height of the steps I had to lean against the walls, just with the tips of my fingers because I do not like touching a wall any more than I do the ground when I happen to pick up a coin.

From the third floor I caught sight of the sun through the landing windows. There was no strength left in it. Not a gleam of light illuminated the dark steps.

When I reached the top storey, I waited for my breathing to become regular again. There was no going any further. The house came to an end there. That I had been able to go all through it like that, even though I did not live there, surprised me.

A ladder to get on to the roof was lying beside a wall. In a door, at the spot where there had been a bolt, there was a wad of paper to prevent draughts. The walls, which were brown up as far as the keyholes and grey above, had been scribbled on. Although his identity might have been discovered, some unknown person had written an obscene word.

I knocked on Lucien's door, in the centre so that the knock would sound more clearly.

I was quite calm. My visit meant so much less than the one my friend had paid the previous day.

The door opened. I saw a curtainless window

looking out on roofs, torn wallpaper, its back white with plaster, a folding bed whose casters Lucien probably turned when it was folded up, a tiled floor which had been sprinkled with a watering can.

I took a step forward. A floor-tile shifted.

A smell of dust and charcoal mingled with the smoke of a single cigarette.

A photograph of Lucien's platoon was still hanging on the wall as well as an old calendar which he kept for the picture.

The ceiling was low. Since I had not had the opportunity to do so for a long time, I raised my hand to touch it. It is silly to admit it, but I like touching ceilings.

'Here you are!' said Lucien. 'I thought you weren't coming.'

His hands were damp. It was his elbow he offered me, raising instead of lowering it.

He was wearing slippers and walking between the splashes of water. He had no jacket. One end of his tie, made of grey fabric, was tucked into his waistcoat. I had the impression that he was wearing two shirts, a flannel vest, a mixture of clean and dirty clothes.

I sat down on a chair without stretchers, the legs of which remained vertical only as long as one did not move it. I hitched up my overcoat. I tugged at my trouser legs, as women always do when they are making fun of men. With my hands on my knees I looked round me.

There was an unfolded newspaper on the table so placed that it could be read during a meal. Some used nails were scattered about. On the back of a chair Lucien had carved his surname, Garin, in capital letters except the G which he did not know how to form.

He passed behind me. Then the room seemed empty as if it belonged to me. It seemed to me that I was poor once again, that I did not know what would become of me.

I thought of Jeanne. That she was busy, that even though I was everything to her, she would not be thinking of me at that moment, touched me.

No, I was not the one who lived there. I was a man now. If anything had happened to me, people, Jeanne, her brother, her friends, would have come to my assistance.

I looked out of the window. Half of the sun had disappeared. I remembered that as a child I would have liked to walk about on the roofs. The chimney-stacks were held steady by wires. My eyes were stinging. I dared not rub them because I had been touching some coppers.

I had kept my coat on. It seemed to me that I ought to have got up, taken it off, hung it up on the door-handle even though it was not high enough, to have talked and laughed.

Lucien had sat down at the head of the bed. He slid his hand under the eiderdown to plump it up on top. When he had finished, he looked at me, lingering over what was sticking out of my pockets: a pencil-case, some papers, a watch–chain, the end of a cigar.

He had been drinking. His cheeks and forehead were flushed and so was the smooth skin of an old scar. He was breathing so slowly that I could see his chest rising and falling. His fingers were not straight. The final sections twisted to one side in a way my father used to dislike.

I was very close to him, so much so that the least movement, even backwards, would have caused me to touch him for a second.

He had not shaved. His beard had grown more thickly on the cheeks, with two strange bare patches at the sides of his chin. In the corners of his eyes there were specks of white which would have slipped out if he had closed them. There was a swelling on one side of the division between his nostrils.

'Does she love you very much, your girlfriend?'

Alone with me, he was trying hard not to be shy, as he had been when we used to see a lot of each other. From certain lines which were not there when his face wore its usual expression, I realized that he envied me.

'You must be very happy in your flat. You have everything you want. It's not as it used to be.'

He spoke with detachment, dropping his eyes before he finished his sentences, but managing always to remind me of my former life.

'Have you known her long?'

He waited for my reply with his mouth half-open, his features suddenly those of an old man, with an anxiety which he tried to disguise by pulling faces for no apparent reason.

I did not reply. He rubbed his hands together and looked at his nails even though they had not been properly looked after, to make me think he had forgotten the question he had just asked.

I was aware of how much he was suffering, of how happy I was in comparison with him. I realized that I ought not, by inviting him, to have pointed out the contrast between his poverty and my easy circumstances.

I tried to comfort him. Without being able to explain why, I guessed that if I told him that Jeanne was a childhood friend, that I had met her again by chance, his misery would be relieved.

'I have known Jeanne for ten years.'

'She is called Jeanne?'

'Yes. It's not a pretty name.'

His expression remained the same. From pure nervousness he had a slight quiver in one cheek which he could not control and which did not affect the flesh. It was the skin which alternately puckered and became smooth again.

'Does she give you money?'

This time I made a defensive movement. It annoyed me that Lucien allowed himself to ask such a question. Through seeing me sympathizing with his sufferings, he thought he could humiliate me as much as he liked.

The sun had vanished leaving no trace of red. Darkness was climbing into the sky, which was still blue.

'She must give you some. Come on, admit it.'

He spoke these words good-naturedly. He was speaking to the unfortunate I had once been. That I was now well-off was for him an accident. It would not last. Even though every day I persuaded myself that I was meant for the life I was now living, that it was the other life which had been an accident, it seemed to me for a second that he was right.

A star twinkled. It was so high up it could not be mistaken for a light on earth. A gust of wind made the window panes rattle. There was a line separating the darkness from the light. Our breath went up as far as this line.

My hands were red. I shifted. I felt a chill run all over my body, along my sides, set off by the movement.

Lucien had stood up. He lit the little stove. I watched him. His Adam's apple moved occasionally as if he had swallowed something. His collar got in the way. Then the Adam's apple returned to its place where there was a mark in the skin.

'You are happy, aren't you, Armand?'

His tongue had not moved. His lips seemed not to have parted. These words, coming out of the darkness, put my ill-humour to flight.

This man had never been happy. For years he had lived alone, anxious, worried about his fragile state of health, despised by the people who knew him by sight. I felt sorry I had failed to make allowances for him.

I looked at him. He was sitting on a chair of which nothing remained of the back except for one upright, smeared with dried glue. He was sitting crosswise, smoking a cigarette.

Jeanne's brother employed four workers. I could have mentioned Lucien to him. He might perhaps have given him work. But I realized I should never dare introduce him to anyone at all after the way he had behaved with Jeanne.

So, because I wanted to do something for him, because the difference in our situations was painful to me, I could not stop myself saying:

'Trust in the future'.

He raised his head without opening his eyes any wider. His chin was lit up by the flames of the stove. From time to time the light slid round to his ears whose pointed shadow lengthened and shortened alternately. His face, remaining impassive under the gleam of light running over it, seemed to me sadder than ever.

'You ought to light the lamp too, Lucien!'

He stood up. His cigarette was so short that he held it between the tips of his fingers when he carried it to his lips. I dared not offer him my silver cigarette case.

Before he lit the lamp, I looked at the sky. It was covered with stars. The moon, caved in on one side because it was not yet full, was shining. The lamplight, passing suddenly over me, blotted it all out.

I turned back. Lucien had sat down near the fire which he knew so well, which he knew would not burn him at that distance.

From time to time a tear gathered in one of his eyes, but each time it was drawn back and disappeared under his eyelid. He had put out his cigarette with his fingers. He was warming his hands, one side after the other,

33

giving more time to the palms because the skin is thicker.

Before so much poverty and simplicity, I was ashamed of living so comfortably. At that moment, if Jeanne had not existed, I should have stood up, I should have taken his hand and said to him:

'I am your only friend.'

The stove had begun to glow so quickly that I remembered that it would be enough to forget the re-fuelling once for it to go out. Lucien was looking after it. There was a network of fine veins on his cheeks. The circles of his eyes cut right into the bridge of his nose as if he had been wearing spectacles. He was round-shouldered. He knew nothing of my impulse towards him. If I had told him about it, he would perhaps have thought I was lying. He had no suspicion of how devoted I was to him. He did not expect anyone to do him a kindness.

There was on his lips not a speck of tobacco, not a drop of moisture, not a crack. They were so smooth and fresh, they were quite different from his face which was covered with a thousand meaningless marks.

He coughed, stuck out his tongue several times, then bent down to riddle the stove. His forehead grew red on the side where he bowed his head.

He sat down squarely on his chair again. I felt the last traces of his breath against my cheek. He turned his eyes towards me. He neither raised nor lowered his head. I was the only human being who took any interest in him. My presence overwhelmed him.

'Come on Lucien, let's get a breath of air. That will cheer us up.'

This time he looked at me. His double chin disappeared. His eyelids lifted. With his eyes encircled with white, his face all attention, he seemed full of

34

guilelessness and anxiety.

I stood up. Once again I touched the ceiling with my hand. I waited for Lucien near the door. Before rising from his chair, he put his garments in order, put on his shoes and looked for his key in his pockets so that once he was on his feet all he had to do was follow me.

## 4

Outside the stars were so numerous that I could see the Great Bear and the Little Bear quite clearly. The weather was cold and dry. The patches of damp on the pavements were covered with thin crinkly ice.

Lucien walked at my side, with his shoulders hunched, comparing his shadow with mine. Occasionally, so that it would be as long, he straightened up and went ahead of me a little.

At a street corner, between the houses, the moon appeared, so close that it seemed to have taken off from the earth.

I did not turn up my overcoat collar because it is shaped to fit. It was about ten minutes short of six o'clock.

We were going along a side-road. The sounds from the neighbouring main street reached our ears through the buildings with two exits. I lit a cigarette. The flame flickered against my eyebrows and made me start back.

Lucien raised one arm to see if his shadow would imitate him. He was one step in front of me. From time to time, without moving his head, he watched me. Although I cannot manage to see more than a quarter circle without turning, Lucien could see almost behind him quite effortlessly.

An oval lamp without a shade, fragile in the windy street, lit up the doorway of a school. An employee of the North-South Railway, whose cap no longer served any purpose, was making his way home on foot.

In front of a wine-shop Lucien stopped.

'This is where I usually go.'

A pale light from the café flooded over us in the street. The condensation on the window-panes was running down inside. The wind was swaying the fringes of the rolled-up blind.

To get in, the door-handle had to be raised instead of being pressed down.

The air in the empty room was warm and steamy. It ran like cold water over my cheeks, into my frozen ears and over my hands when I took them out of my pockets. The stove was out. On a folded sack a cat was asleep with its head lower than its body.

I sat down. Lucien, watching all my movements carefully, was trying hard to interpret them so he could anticipate them. He had thought I would drink at the counter. He was already leaning on it. Fearing that I had noticed what he was up to, he blushed.

When his face had recovered its pallor, he came and sat down beside me.

With his ring finger, which was just as agile as the others, he wiped away a drop on the wooden table.

The proprietress of the café came up to us. She smiled like an old comrade. I have often noticed, since I was demobilized, that certain people have the same expression as soldiers I have known. I used to ask them if they did not have relations who served in certain regiments on the Eastern Front. They always answered in the negative. So, although these likenesses continue to surprise me, I now take care not to ask any questions.

We ordered the same apéritif. We were alone. On the walls there were some metal advertisements and a postal calendar still showing the months that had gone.

Lucien was looking at a hole in the floor. A knot had come out of one of the planks. The hole went through to the cellar.

He was motionless. His folded right hand rested on the table. He was dreaming. I picked up my glass. He was holding his own so clumsily that I had to touch it on the foot to chink glasses.

Seeing him like that, sad and tired, I wanted to tell him how much I felt for him in his sufferings in spite of what it looked like. I wanted him to get rid of the impression he was forming of me. He would have loved me if he had been able to guess what I really thought of him. And as I could not manage to make him understand by my words, I tried very hard to make my gestures show what I was like. I was straight-forward. I avoided behaving in the ways I affected when I was with Jeanne. I made all my movements slowly so he would have time to copy them.

I called him. Before turning round he finished looking at something. I took his hand.

'Lucien!'

Even though he was not facing me directly, he looked me in the eye.

At that moment I almost wished that we should only be separated for the night, that each of us should go to his room and meet again just the same the next day.

He had just taken a drink. A drop of liquid was sliding down the side of his glass. He was waiting for this liquid to form a mouthful.

I was nervous. A fine sweat, scarcely damper than if a tongue had licked it, covered my forehead. I was afraid that some noise, some unforeseen occurrence, might break the bond which was being established between Lucien and me. I was aware from the dryness of my lips, from the chill of my cheeks which felt as if they were hardly part of my face, that I was pale. I had not crossed my legs so that my feet could get warm better, so that the blood could reach them more quickly.

I squeezed Lucien's hand hard, as I do when I am trying to make someone's joints hurt for a joke.

He looked at me without changing the rhythm of his breathing or blinking at all. I could feel his pulse throbbing more strongly and rapidly because I was squeezing his hand.

Then, in obedience to some interior command which I have never been able to explain, unless it was that I simply wanted to humble myself, to show myself in another light, to put myself on Lucien's level, I murmured:

'I am not happy.'

I waited. He looked at me without surprise. All was silence around us. A vehicle passed in the street. I stopped listening to it even before it had stopped making a noise.

It seemed to me that I had only to speak. The man next to me was listening. He would give me advice. He would not envy me. I had a friend. If Jeanne left me, he would comfort and support me.

'Lucien . . . I am not happy.'

He did not move. Something creaked behind him. He did not look round. Faced with such apathy, I almost altered the meaning of my words by adding something, by adding: 'When you do not speak to me, when I am cold.'

'You do not know, Lucien, how I sometimes long to be free, to do what I want, to go home when I wish. Jeanne is very nice, but I think that before, when we spent our time together, I was happier.'

I had forgotten I was holding his hand. He pulled it free. I felt as if something had been taken away from me, as if the hand ought to have waited for me to release it.

Lucien's face brightened. His eyes grew narrow. He smiled. But his mouth, which did not change, made the smile very sad.

My admission had roused him from his torpor. From the way he held his head, his half-closed eyes and the set of his nose, I could see that my words had got through to him, that he was pleased at the thought of my becoming his friend again.

Then in a gesture of affection I took him by the shoulders, pressed him against me without looking at him, with my head thrown back, so that this impulsive movement should display none of the signs of love between a man and a woman.

We stayed like that for a moment. Then he freed himself. I was embarrassed. Suddenly it seemed to me that I had gone too far, that I had been too trusting, that I was still lacking in experience.

I saw an alarm clock on a shelf. The hands covered the second dial. It was half-past six. It would not be long before Jeanne went home.

I stood up. Lucien had crossed his legs in a way that I should have found very tiring.

I realized that his life was independent of mine. If I were not there he would have carried on with his concerns in just the same way. He was a stranger. He would have been incapable of sacrificing himself for me. He despised all the interest I took in him. He thought only of himself. I suspected that even his shyness was feigned.

I stood by the counter and waited for him to join me. But he did not move. He was surprised that I had got up like that, suddenly, without warning. He was annoyed: people who go to cafés like to have time to finish their second drink. I was aware that it was so. All the same it did not worry me. On the contrary, for no reason, I almost wished I had done something which would have annoyed him more.

I could picture the sort of life he led. It disgusted me

deeply. The thoughts which went through my mind, because they were always the same, wearied me. After all, I had no need of him. Jeanne loved me. The course of my life was unfolding peacefully. Why should I then abase myself before this man who, if he had been in my place, would not have put himself out?

As far as Lucien was concerned, I felt deeply indifferent. He had only to follow his path and I would follow mine. The memory of his lamentations made me feel I should stand up for myself. He begrudged me my happiness. He envied me.

Everything good in me gave way to such anger that I would have liked to push him away, knock over the table, take a kick at a chair and leave.

I restrained myself. He had not risen. With both hands on the table and his shoulders unencumbered by my arm, like those of a woman who has just taken off her fur wrap, he was staring at me.

Then he went on drinking. He ignored my anger just as he had ignored my earlier impulsiveness. He had put his glass down and was twiddling the stem between his fingers as I sometimes do with a single lock of my hair.

So he too, at certain times, needed to twiddle something between his fingers, a soft bit of bread or some hair.

'Come on Lucien, get up. I must go. Jeanne will be expecting me for dinner.'

He obeyed with unaccustomed haste, so that for the first time, I despised him. He was dimly aware that something unusual had happened.

Now he seemed to me a man without dignity. If I had struck him he would not have defended himself.

We went out into the street. The darkness, like the light, made me blink. On each side of us, equidistant, was a street-lamp. The contractors had imagined they were placed so that the light from them would be continuous. Nevertheless, we were in shadow.

I waited for him to close the door. He could not manage it because the latch was stuck in the lock.

At last he joined me. I had taken several paces without turning round. I was so far from him that I had almost gone.

'Take me the shortest way. I am in a hurry.'

He considered. I could see that he was mentally setting the streets end to end, weighing them up so that the various routes would be straight lines which he could compare more easily.

He had lowered the brim of his hat to keep off the cold. Although his overcoat was single-breasted, he held it crossed over. He had put up his collar, which was hardly any higher than a jacket collar and gave him an air of poverty.

'Come on, let's go.'

He went with me as far as a square which was scattered with traffic-islands. The pavements and the light of the street lamps trembled as the omnibuses went by. In the centre there was an ornamental pool. The black water was too shallow. The pillars which supported the bronze Tritons could be seen.

I stopped.

'Lucien, I shall leave you here, I know where I am.'

A lighted shop-window showed him up from head to foot. The cracks which intersected his lips had gone as if he had moistened them with his tongue. With his hands in his pockets and his arms tense and turned inwards, he looked as if he wanted to imitate someone with knock-knees.

'Goodbye, Lucien.'

He did not take his hands out of his pockets. I hesitated to leave him without shaking hands, because afterwards I should have felt him near me. Even though I was alone, I should have been tied to him. He would have been consistently present at my side as if we had not finished a conversation.

Nevertheless I did leave him like that, without offering him my hand. He was watching me going away as if I were not departing on foot.

It was a relief to be free, to have the witness of my unhappy past no longer beside me. I walked quickly, feeling momentarily furious when I had to mark time behind people who were dawdling, stopping from time to time in front of shop-windows where the new hats reminded me of my birthday and name-day.

I went into a real café in order to forget the wine-shop I had been in earlier. The mirrors made it seem so huge that I was surprised for a moment to find myself at the end of a room.

It was cocktail time. I sat on a blue metal chair with splayed legs so that the chairs did not take up much room when they were stacked after closing time. I have always been struck by inventions of that sort, the safety razor, the washing-machine, which are so simple and yet no one had previously thought of them. I too am trying to make a discovery for which I could apply for a patent, because it seems to me that that is the only way in which I could get rich.

The ceiling was studded with golden stars with rays of glass. The plate-glass and copper doors reflected regular but not dazzling beams of light as they swung to and fro. There was writing on the windows which could be seen back to front from inside the café. I could only make out the words of one syllable, though Jeanne could have read everything easily as she often embroidered initials.

I was alone at my table, I lowered the flaps of the table so that no one could sit near me.

Soon afterwards a clock struck. I looked round for it

as I had not heard the first strokes. It was gone seven o'clock when I found it.

Jeanne was waiting for me.

5

The next morning I awoke earlier than usual, although there had been no noise or nightmare to account for it, with a sudden lucidity which prevented me from going to sleep again. I rubbed my eyes. They made a little damp noise, like a kiss.

It was not yet nine o'clock. My tongue was sore because I had smoked too much the day before. I had no strength in my hands. My handkerchief was no longer under the pillow. Jeanne was still asleep. From her light breathing, the trembling of her long eyelashes and the way her flesh quivered I was aware that the least movement would have aroused her.

I did not move. I wanted to be alone until I had collected my thoughts.

The room was submerged in semi–darkness. The window was hidden by a curtain stained at the top. In the places where the fabric was worn I could see the daylight through it.

Suddenly Jeanne opened her eyes. All at once, as if the light had gone right inside her head, her face brightened. She threw off the bedclothes. Her night-gown was wound round her body. I reached for her hand. I felt down her arm to find it. I squeezed it. I hurt her. Jeanne is more sensitive in the morning than in the evening. She does not like me to touch her when she is waking up. She needs to regain consciousness on her own. This lasts for several minutes, during which I have to leave her alone so that she has time to come to herself, to think about the various parts of herself, one at a time, because she is afraid some disease may have struck her in the night, just as people fear someone may have died during their absence.

I put my lips to her forehead and not her cheeks so that I did not have to kiss her twice. I raised my head. She slipped her arm around my neck and hugged me against her. We did not speak because in the morning we were too lazy to speak the least word. By tacit agreement we did not even say good morning to each other.

We stayed like that for a long while. I stroked her breasts, which are not sensitive, her hips, and her shoulders, which were moist with cream, avoiding the beauty spot which hurts her.

She had closed her eyes again without having looked at herself in a looking-glass. As she lay beside me, her true nature was revealed. She no longer had to force herself to appear womanly and attractive, because, feeling me against her, she was confident she was so.

I sat up in bed after having leaned heavily on her chest for a joke. She called me a tease. I knew that my pranks amused her, even when she was their victim, from the very moment that I was keeping a straight face.

Every morning I sit like that, because when I am lying down I never know if I have a migraine. I was all right. There was just a slight heaviness, more like numbness than anything else, above my eyes. I stood up. The bedside rug is so small that it slipped on the parquet when I put a foot on the floor.

I opened the curtains. That is what I always do first. As long as I do not know what the weather is like, it seems to me that the previous day has not come to an end. The looking-glass on the wardrobe stopped being a patch of brightness in the gloom. The chairs had cumbersome shadows because of the clothes piled up on them.

46

I had lived in one room for so long that it gave me great pleasure to walk from one room to another. I opened and closed the doors. I wondered briefly if I should put on one of Jeanne's dresses. She liked me to dress as she did and to pretend to be a woman. But it was too cold.

I went to our door to fetch the paper with its somewhat stale news that had already appeared in the evening editions. Having glanced through the headlines, I folded it up again so that Jeanne would know it was that morning's paper without looking at the date.

Then I went into the dressing-room which was also used as a box room.

As soon as I was ready I returned to Jeanne. She was asleep again with her face hidden in her arm. Her hair, which was as long at her temples as elsewhere, was not covering her ears. She had her wedding-ring on her finger. She never took it off so that I could not read the inscription which her husband, who had been killed in the war, had had engraved inside it.

I picked up my jacket which had been put on the chair with the back shaped most like my shoulders. I made a slight noise so that Jeanne would wake up. She did not move. So I tip-toed out, avoiding the blocks of parquet which creaked.


The weather had changed. Clouds were chasing across the sky. I was glad. Nothing pleases me so much in the morning as weather which is different from that of the day before. It brings back memories, as a smell from the past or an early fruit does.

The air was so clear that I could see insects coming and had time to close my eyes. The sounds around me were not too loud for my ears, even when I passed very close to them.

A cloud hid the sun. I did not mind: it was moving so quickly across the sky that the sun would soon appear again.

I went along a broad avenue covered with earth which looked as if it had been laid there, like the earth in roof-gardens. I breathed the cool air as slowly as I possibly could. Great bare branches were bending with the wind, as flexible as they were in summer. Plane-tree fruits were dropping from them and smashing into fragments on the ground.

The movement of the clouds drove me to exert myself, to hasten my steps, to think about aeroplanes which could go from one to another and to wonder whether the pilots could see clearly as they passed through them. My features were still heavy with sleep and my finger-nails soft because they had been wet.

In the distance rose the houses, sometimes in sunlight, sometimes in a misty drizzle like distant rain. It was rainbow weather. From time to time, as happens in flat open country, great shafts of light, hazy with mist, fell from the clouds when the sun was behind them.

High up on a church I could see the blackened hands of a clock without glass. I did not know if it was ten to eleven or five to ten.

I had no intention of going to see Lucien. Nevertheless, without thinking about it, I avoided the streets which would have taken me away from his house. I was sorry I had been so short with him the day before. I wanted to talk about myself, to tell him that I had an impulsive nature, but that I was really very kind.


I found Lucien in bed. His muscular arms were bare. Their whiteness surprised me because I was used to the dark colouring of his face. It was colder in his room

48

than outside. It was just as untidy in the morning as it had been in the evening.

He had put a box on a chair so that it would be high enough for a bedside table. The glass of the lamp was black. He had left his tie inside his collar. A smell of cooking, which had crept under the door, hung about the room.

For a moment I thought of going away again. But he had sat up in bed. He held the counterpane round his body, like a towel after a bath. He had rolled up his sleeves to sleep, removed the studs from the neckband of his shirt for fear of losing them while he was asleep and of not knowing where to start looking for them.

'I'll wait for you downstairs. Perhaps you would rather I was not here while you got dressed.'

'No, stay.'

He yawned so protracted a yawn that a drop of saliva fell from his mouth. The sun was turning the window-frame golden. I did not know if it had just reached there or if it had already come and was now going again.

With one hand in front of him, like a statue, Lucien climbed out of bed at the top, as if it had been a sleeping-bag, so that he did not disarrange it. His legs were still marked by the elastic of his socks. He pulled on his trousers standing on the bed, so that the legs should not drag in the pink dust of the tiled floor. Then he jumped to the ground and, with his feet bare, came and went about the room, keeping well away from the chairs in order not to hurt himself.

I had sat down near the window, which I dared not open because Lucien had stripped to the waist. The wound in the side which he had received during the war and which he had shown me two years before, simply by uncovering it, seemed smaller, in the middle of his trunk. I could not take my eyes off it. I had often thought about it while I was talking to Lucien. It distanced me from him. Now, because I saw it so clearly and had got to know it better, Lucien was closer to me.

He was washing himself, with his eyes closed so that the soap did not sting them, and his head held straight so that the water did not get into his ears. His hair was tangled. He parted it with a comb which had the teeth missing at one side.

'I came to surprise you.'

He turned round, the soap in his hand, without squeezing it, so that it should not slip between his fingers.

'To surprise me?'

'Yes, I wanted to see you again after what we said yesterday. I was unkind.'

He could not remember. He tried to recollect.

'What time?'

'Yesterday evening, before I left you.'

This time he remembered everything, but did not understand that I could be sorry about anything. Meanwhile, feeling that he ought to seem moved, he said:

'I wanted to see you too. But I should never have dared to come to your house.'

Silence followed these words. The thought that he had found it possible even to think of coming to my house displeased me.

He went to the bed. His drying foot-prints remained in front of his dressing-table. He picked up his socks, turned them the right way round because they got inside out when he took them off, like mine.

Before putting on his shirt, he thumped himself on the chest. He had been proud of the sound it made ever since I had told him it was a sign of good health.

When he was dressed, he asked me to brush his back.

There was no shortage of brushes. He had brought a dozen back from the army. He still had five or six of them. He had sold the others because they were all similar, because he had calculated that half would last him for the rest of his life.

We had not spoken for a while. He was making his bed, tucking it in just as well on the wall side. I lit my first cigarette of the day.

Suddenly someone knocked at the door.

I had kept my hat on. I took it off.

## 6

Lucien looked towards the door just as the knocking came again, more loudly this time, as if he were asleep.

He hesitated to make any noise.

He did not move so that his shape, seen through the keyhole, should not betray him.

A period of time had passed equal to that which had separated the first two knocks. After a slight delay, the knocking would be renewed.

Two shadows, which our eyes could not hold on to, shifted under the door.

It was perhaps a postman and, in spite of myself, I looked round for a bottle of ink.

Fear swept over me, like the fear I experience in rooms with windows that are not near a drain-pipe and from which there appears to be no means of escape in a fire.

Somebody knocked again, with the fist this time, and more loudly than before.

Lucien leaned towards me. It was a habit of his to speak into the ear. Because he was so ignored he unconsciously needed to address the senses themselves. When he showed me anything, he held it so close to my eyes that I could not see it very well. When he wanted me to smell anything, he pushed it close enough to my nose to dirty it, without however having any idea of playing a trick on me.

'It's my sister Marguerite. Shall I open the door?'

This surprised me. I did not know that he had a sister. He had never spoken of her. I thought no one visited him.

'Yes, do.'

He turned the key, just once. Like me, he thought that one turn of the key would lock just as well as two.

A girl appeared.

Seeing me, she hesitated to come in. Her hand was on the door-knob. The action of the door was too simple to be adapted to the doubts which assailed her. Nevertheless she pushed it to and fro as she passed from confidence to fear.

Finally, because it would have been silly to go, she came into the room, without pushing the door too far open, because she must have been used to slipping in and out.

She stopped immediately. She was not carrying a bag. Her hands were trying to conceal themselves in the pockets of her dress, which were too small, as pockets in women's clothes always are. Her hair, with its invisible combs, had darkened with age. Nothing could obliterate the freckles from her face, shorten her nose, make her pale eyes larger or lengthen her receding chin, which left her lower lip unsupported.

She was wearing a coat with the shoulder-seams hanging down over her arms, floppy turned-back cuffs which hid her hands when she curled them up, and buttons which came undone of their own accord.

'You did not tell me you were coming,' said Lucien.

He seemed to have forgotten I was there. Confronted with Marguerite he had become aggressive and ill-natured without experiencing the least embarrassment at changing thus before my eyes.

For a second it seemed to me that he was a hypocrite, because he had in no way blamed me, who, like his sister, had appeared without warning. But I attributed this attitude to the friendship he professed for me.

Marguerite did not reply. All she had with her was a handkerchief, which she was crumpling so much that it would have stayed in a ball if she had put it down.

Lucien had finished getting dressed. His collar was fastened by a pin. A lock of hair which had been pushed back formed a little bunch and from time to time he smoothed it into place.

The alarm-clock showed midday, midday so that the hands looked as if they had become stuck together.

Marguerite occasionally glanced round at the bed, the dressing-table and whatever she would have had to tidy had she lived in the room.

We were motionless, all three of us, not daring to take a step for fear of being embarrassed.

Lucien wanted to open the window. It was stiff and he showed his annoyance. Marguerite, who was smaller and slighter than I, was waiting for a kind word. She had not stirred since she had come in, so that the fact of her visit was all that there was of it. Because it was so obvious that she had taken a decision, she was abashed. Like a child she was afraid that circumstances which she could not foresee because of her youth would reveal her solitary thoughts.

Suddenly Lucien addressed her roughly:

'I have told you before that I do not want you to come here without warning me. The next time I shall not open the door. But you are so stubborn. Just go away. You can see I have a gentleman with me.'

She lowered her eyes. She had folded her hands over her stomach. I felt like intervening, but dared not because it was so clear that Lucien, who had become angry about his sister's lack of manners so that I could not possibly defend her, was terrified I would say something.

'I have had enough . . . Get out.'

This time Marguerite started. Her hands flew apart. From the curious shape of her cheeks I guessed that, in order not to cry, she was cautiously biting her tongue, as near the end as possible, where it was most sensitive.

I could restrain myself no longer. I moved towards her. This astonished her so much that she stopped biting her tongue and her top lip lifted, revealing her front teeth. She clasped her hands again, then slid them slowly into her sleeves as if into a hiding-place.

'Do stay; it will be all right.'

She looked at me, wide-eyed. No hint of red dimmed their clarity. They looked as if they were emerging from water. The corners, clear and pink, did not encroach upon the whites.

She turned her head. Lucien had put himself between us. Since there was only a step between Marguerite and me, he was touching both of us.

'You are taking sides with her?'

I realized that he was going to make an issue of his authority as a member of the family, that this was sacred to him and that, if it was by-passed, he would have flown into a passion which any witness would judge reasonable.

'Oh, no, Lucien.'

However he went on:

'I am her brother. I know better than anyone how to bring her up.'

He took me by the arm, leaning towards me, and, a couple of steps away, said in my ear:

'Leave her alone.'


We went out. He had put his hat on one side. Going down the stairs, with his hands in his pockets, he looked as if he was outside already.

It was colder. The sun had gone. The sky was covered with mist, and if one looked at it for long enough, white gashes could be seen scattered all over it.

Beyond a few houses was a café. We went in. A calendar was hanging on a round pillar. A single street directory lay on the bar. Although it was daylight I noticed that, at night, the room was not lit by electricity.

We settled ourselves at a marble table which was screwed to the floor. It was not possible to move it in order to get into the corner. I sat down close to a window, so that eventually I was leaning against it.

Through the curtains the street could be seen, as white as if it had snowed. Buses kept passing by, always in the same direction, as they came back along a wider street.

Lucien had not sat down. He was thinking. He was not sure what he ought to do. Suddenly he went towards the door, as if to make sure it was properly closed. For a moment he stood motionless. Then he opened it, saying simply:

'I'll be back.'

Marguerite called him, each time more feebly, though the distance was growing. I no longer existed in her eyes. She had both her hands clenched, as if I had to guess in which of them was the longer straw.

Without pinching her lips together, she bit her tongue again. She was no longer fighting off tears, but hysterics.

The door had closed all by itself.

Lucien passed in front of the windows without trying to see us, hastily put a cigarette to his lips so that we could tell how little he cared, and then disappeared behind the vertical line of the wall.

She pressed a hand against her left cheek. For a moment she hid her nose, without reflecting how ugly a face is without one. Then, giving way to her nerves, she pushed her fingers into her flesh, and then her palm, which was stronger, as if that might be enough to alter her features. In her distress, to strike and injure herself were not enough. She was attacking her face itself because, by obliterating herself she wanted to destroy the last part of her which retained any dignity.

I could not guess what lay behind that pain. I wanted to question her. She stammered out:

'He'll hit me . . . he won't forgive me.'

She kept her eyes on the curtainless door, the only point from where it was possible to see the street clearly.

She was hoping that her brother would come back, that he had gone away in order to frighten her. She was waiting for him with her eyes, her ears, her motionless arms, dimly aware of the growing distance between her and him as time passed.

A step behind her, at a spot where Lucien would not have been unless he had gone round the block and come in the back way, made her turn round, a silhouette behind the curtains made her half rise to her feet and press her forehead against the window, angry that she could not put her head through it and mildly surprised that transparent glass was rigid and would not shape itself to her face.

I wanted to comfort her. It seemed to me that Lucien was quite heartless to treat a child like that. Nevertheless I felt no contempt for him. His hardness brought me closer to him. It proved to me that he was without affection.

But Marguerite had nobody either. Nobody loved her. I was the only one to take an interest in her. And even while I was hoping that Lucien would not come back, I pitied her.

I watched her secretly. She was aware of it, but dared not put an end to my little game by suddenly turning to face me.

We stayed like that for several minutes. Locks of

hair, short like a man's, curled on her neck. When she was sitting down her body had lost its stiffness. She bowed her head. Her clothing was still puffed out more, but her shoulders inside it were rounder.

Suddenly she stood up. For a moment, in spite of the difference of sex, her expression resembled her brother's. I was afraid she would go away without a word, that I would have to catch up with her, to follow a few paces behind her.

But she looked straight at me. It was a direct gaze. I felt that I had made a mistake.

'Shall we go?' I asked, standing up in my turn.

As if she was afraid of being surprised, she replied with a single nod of the head, of the kind the meaning of which could at the last moment be changed by a look.

At the door she stood aside so that I could go out first.

Outside a child was running past. The wind was blowing so hard that I raised my hand to my hat. The hands of a clock showed one o'clock. The face was empty like the streets. Although there was no sun, the occasional passers-by had shadows, so light that they seemed to be gliding over ground of dazzling whiteness.

In her wide dress, Marguerite was walking at the same pace as I. She was showing me the sort of consideration which I ought to have been showing her. Thinking that Lucien was perhaps watching her, as she had recently been watching him, she looked at the cafés, only managing to see inside them when the reflections scattered, exposing the glass of the windows.

I wanted to speak, to comfort her, but was only able to ask if I might accompany her.

She did not even turn her head. The wind was

tangling her hair, turning the little broken veins in her cheeks blue and making her skirt flap behind her.

'If you like.'

We reached a square with a white statue in the middle of it. We were bathed in a flood of light which did not come from the sky and which the clouds were too high to conceal.

A single drop fell from the sky. Others followed it. It was going to rain.

I entertained myself by imagining that the drops were the bullets from a rifle and that I could avoid them by zigzagging about. One of them pierced my hat, another my foot.

The air was full of dust which, when the wind dropped suddenly, fell like rain.

We quickened our pace. Marguerite could walk as quickly as I. It was still not raining. We were going along a narrow street, which was paved and tarred alternately. Drops kept on falling here and there, without making much of a splash. It was still weather for sitting on benches.

We had arrived in front of an old hotel with a door which could not be mistaken for that of the neighbouring building because the wall had been repainted.

The wind had closed the left-hand shutter of each window. The sign was stained with splashes of plaster.

Marguerite had stopped. She offered me her hand. She held it straight out, as if she were about to pull a glove off it.

'Are you going home already?'

She closed her eyes, bowed her head and took a step sideways because I was still holding her hand. She was nervous. For the first time she exhibited a girl's newly-acquired shyness. I was aware that she was no longer thinking of her brother. She was deeply disturbed by having me, a man, at the door of her home.

59

'I must go in.'

She drew back, with her arm stretched out so that I still had her hand. I squeezed it, making an effort to hold it like that, as in a game.

But soon I was holding only the tips of her fingers.

At last, because somebody was passing, I let her go. There was immediately a wide gap between us. She faced me for one second more. I saw her from head to foot. The hand I had released made a graceful movement, more graceful than the other hand which had never been a prisoner.

At the moment when she turned, when she was taking another step, I murmured:

'May I come with you?'

She entered the corridor without replying. Before she disappeared I saw her taking smaller steps, so that she could walk as quickly in the passage, which was narrow and short, as in the streets at my side.

I withdrew to the opposite pavement and, without raising my head too much or attracting attention, I watched the hotel windows for several minutes.

7

The same evening after dinner, so that I could go out, I pretended to need to be alone, a wish that Jeanne respected without understanding, persuading herself, with the thought always at the back of her mind that it was necessary to make sacrifices in the present in order to be happy in the future, that a woman ought never to oppose a man's wishes if she wants to keep him.

Several times during the afternoon I had thought about Marguerite and experienced a certain difficulty in breathing when after being distracted my attention returned to her.

The damp pavements, as black as if they were new and with white stones here and there, were gleaming. The wind had dried things up. Taken by surprise, shot through with moonlight, the clouds remained motionless, as if frozen.

As I walked I tried to imagine Marguerite's room. Sometimes it seemed large to me, sometimes small. Since I was sure that none of them was anything like the reality, I kept on picturing new ones so that, among all those rooms, there might be at least one which would be something like that belonging to Lucien's sister.

Fine bark which would have disintegrated before one could peel it off covered the great branches of the trees. The street lamps, like little fortresses, were crowned with battlements.

Soon I found myself in front of the hotel near which Marguerite had left me a few hours before. The illuminated sign was switched on. The door, which was so small that anyone could have closed it, was ajar, as it might be at night when a resident forgot to push it to.

I went into the narrow corridor which was decorated with a long mirror in several pieces, just as at the time when it was invented.

The owner of the hotel was reading over the names of the residents in the police book. From a sense of delicacy I only asked him what floor Marguerite's room was on. When he took off his spectacles to look at me, it seemed to me that he could no longer see me.

I climbed the staircase which had such small landings that the steps of the following storey began before I had had time to rest. Everything had been newly decorated. Nevertheless everything revealed the age of the building: the rough walls under the smooth paint, the plates of the meters which had been repainted without being opened, the grooves on the doors, the keys hanging from the locks and the gas lighting.

I was not excited. When I reached Marguerite's door, which I had found at once in the gloom, I hesitated to knock, being suddenly afraid that Lucien had lied to me, that he might be there, that that child might be his mistress.

I listened, turning my head from one side to the other because I always forget which of my ears hears better.

No light or noise reached me. In a neighbouring room a man and a woman were talking in low voices.

I took off my hat in advance. I moved my cigarettes from one pocket to another. It took me several seconds to find the right place. I knocked softly, as one does in the evening.

In the darkness I tried to straighten my parting. It

was shorter than I thought. I put it right with a finger, trying to restore its beginning through my tangled hair.

Marguerite opened the door so quickly that she saw me lowering my hand without knowing where it came from.

She started. I had put one foot forward so that she could not close the door again. However I dared not go in. Her hair, which was still in plaits, hung down her back and, like that of all women, disappointed me by its lack of length. She was trembling. Her emotion came partly from the respect I inspired in her, so that she was uncertain, torn between the desire to close the door and to open it wide.

At last she stood aside, then pushed the door to gently.

With short rapid movements, as though she was wearing a dressing-gown which she had to hold fastened at the same time, she busied herself hiding linen and plates, out of an obscure modesty about white things.

Although the room was small, it was cold. The window, set straight in a sloping wall, was shut. The bed, tucked in carefully at the foot, was not touching the wall because of the damp. Useless objects cluttered up the furniture. Like me when I lived on my own, she could not bear to throw away boxes and bottles which bore witness to the spending of money.

The room was lit by a lamp.

Marguerite went to get a chair, dragging it behind her like a child playing trains. I sat down. I was embarrassed. It suddenly seemed to me that I had gone too far, that I had taken advantage of the impression I made to visit that child in the evening.

She sat down in her turn. We were face to face without a table between us.

She was wearing a camisole and a flannel petticoat, because of the respect poor people have for flannel, and on her feet she had slippers which had been turned into mules because she was too lazy to bend down and undo them.

We stayed like that for a long moment, so long that a resident had time to climb the whole staircase. She was calmer than when I had left her. She was looking around furtively, for fear of having left some object she wished to hide from me on a piece of furniture. Even if she had suddenly seen one she would not have dared to rise but would have been obliged to make excuses to justify its presence.

A voice, which was broken off just before it could be understood, sounded in a neighbouring room. Then a door banged with such force that various objects shook, the lamp smoked for a second and we blinked.

Our eyes, in the middle of what surrounded them, met as we opened them.

A tiny noise rose from my feet when I moved my toes, as I did when I was poor to feel whether they were wet. My temples, which were so thin, could hear the pulsing of my arteries, my nostrils could hear the air they drew through them. The noises came only from myself, from my hands when I clenched them, from my mouth when I tasted my saliva which was still flavoured with coffee, from my ears themselves, which my eyes sometimes made creak as they looked down.

Marguerite must be aware of the same noises coming from herself. Like me, she was on the watch for them and, as she was shyer, dreaded them.

I made the senseless gesture of moving my chair closer to hers. She seemed not to notice. With her head bowed and her hands joined, but not as in a picture with one exactly against the other, she was thinking.

64

Before such submissiveness, weakness and poverty, I was overcome by pity. Nevertheless she was happy. She said nothing. She was content to savour my presence without looking for its cause or its purpose.

I moved my chair still nearer. I would have liked to speak to her in a low voice, to be close to her to make her like other women, to teach her to defend herself. But I kept quiet. She could not understand all the friendship I felt for her. I was for her the man she had been waiting for without knowing it, who had to come one day. New feelings were rising within her, very different from mine.

In a movement of which I was only half in control, I took hold of her two joined hands, wishing that they would part, that I should have only one of them, so it would be smaller than mine, so that I could caress the palm. But on the contrary she squeezed them more tightly together. Then I looked at her arms. They were whiter on the side next to her body, the side the sun never reached.

Marguerite did not defend herself. Her lower lip trembled from time to time as if, in her emotion, she forgot to control it.

I examined her fingers one by one, holding only the one I was looking at, lingering over the longer ones as if they deserved more attention.

I bent over her hands, not particularly in order to be able to stroke them along their length, absent-mindedly, touched by the child's joyless life.

Men seemed to her the owners of so many talents that, although I remained bending forward, she cannot have dared look at me for fear that I might be aware of it by some means of which she was ignorant.

Then, without thinking, because of the tenderness which overwhelmed me, I placed my lips on her fingers.

She spread them apart so that I could not kiss them, jumped up and hid in a corner of the room behind a trunk which she could have dodged round if I had pursued her.

I had stood up.

She eyed me for a moment from head to foot. Then she came up to me and held out the very hand she had just withdrawn from me.

'Don't be cross with me.'

I took her arm. As we were standing up, it would have seemed we were about to part if I too had given her my hand.

With her head bowed, she seemed to be committing some fault. I wanted to hug her against me. She defended herself gently and made me let go with the same movement which, in the theatre, is presented as so violent.

Free once more, she sat down on the bed and, so that I should not be angry, seized my hand and laid the back of it against her cheek because she remembered that the palm is placed against all sorts of things.

In my turn I sat down close to her. I tried to make her raise her head, as one does a child, by putting a finger under her chin.

If I had withdrawn my imprisoned hand, which I could easily have done as the palm was towards me, it would have made everything collapse like scaffolding. I kept quite still, as if a movement would have spoiled a photograph.

At last, I put my hand on her waist. The curve of my wrist before it was supported seemed ludicrous.

My face was close to hers. Her lips were trembling more delicately than a man's would have done. She was trying hard not to oppose me, because to her mind I was the one she was destined to love, who would appear only once. She believed the opportunity would come. She was always afraid of not recognizing it. The unusual provided a touch-stone. So, because my presence in her room was so much out of the ordinary, she felt certain that I was the opportunity for which she had been waiting for so long.

I was facing her so that it would be my forehead, where the skin was softer than the rest of my face, which would touch her cheeks first. I was calm. No desire drove me to move any closer to her. Nevertheless I held her against me, not tightly, because I dared not put my arm right round her.

'What are you doing?'

She was still not protecting herself. Suddenly, calculatingly, she moved away from me. Like all women, she thought that later I should reproach her for having given way too easily. But it was quite plain that the change was deliberate. She was well enough aware of the situation not to dare persist in this behaviour, for fear of trying my patience and of being obliged afterwards to humiliate herself so that I did not leave her.

So, pitying such anxiety, I kissed her on the mouth.

She kept it shut. My kiss made no sound. It was only my lips that were placed on hers.

In the presence of that child, who was torn between her virtue and the desire not to offend me, I was seized with remorse.

I stood up, but remained stooping, with my face on a level with hers, so that she should not think I was trying to get away from her. In spite of myself, because I was bent double, I shook my head, as if I were trying to amuse a child.

She looked at me with astonishment, then, with her eyes, indicated a place beside her.

I was aware that I ought not to stay, because otherwise I should have allowed her to cherish hopes which I should afterwards have had to dissipate. I straightened up.

'I must go, Marguerite, it is late.'

It was the first time I had spoken her Christian name.

I had not looked at my watch. I told her it was eleven o'clock. She believed it as if I were incapable of being mistaken.

She stood up. With her legs against the bed, ready to fall backwards at the least loss of balance, she stared at me.

She was thinking that it was not the time that should have made us part, but a complete understanding.

Having uttered a few pleasant generalities, I prepared to leave. For her, these words were the same as if I had remained at her side.

I took my hat, pulled it into shape and, although I do not like wearing a hat indoors, put it on my head.

She did not go near the door, either to open it or to block my way.

As I was about to go out, she ran to me, murmured a few words and began to sob.

'Cheer up, Marguerite, I shall come and see you again. I must go.'

I nearly said that Jeanne was waiting for me, accustomed as I was to take my leave of everyone with these words.

She grew calm and drew back a little. I opened the door, just enough to be able to get through, so that the darkness of the landing should not emphasize her distress. Once I was outside I stuck my head foolishly into the opening and smiled at her.

She did not respond to my smile and, before I disappeared, quickly busied herself with some tidying to show me what she would be doing when I had left her.


Every other street–light was out.

Clouds, as light as in the morning, were passing across the sky, from east to west this time. The moon was only a slender crescent. There was still a pale mark in the place where it had been when it was full.

I thought about Marguerite.

I was sorry then that I had let myself go so far as to kiss her. She might tell her brother everything. This idea, which his estrangement made possible, tormented me. Yet so uncertain was my state of mind that at certain moments I no longer suspected it.

A taxi, lit up like a cab, passed close by me. Because of a childish fear of prowlers I was walking well away from the walls.

I could not stop thinking about the visit I had just paid. One by one all my actions appeared before my eyes.

It suddenly occurred to me that I had deceived Jeanne, that she would find out and that she and I would have a terrible scene.

I started. I only had to deny it. There was no witness to contradict me. I was even more credible than Marguerite.

I went into a café where half the lights were out. I had a beer. I asked the time as I had been taught to do when I was a child. It was not late.

I could have mooched about for a bit longer as I had on other evenings. But I had the impression that I had been away from Jeanne for many hours, that she had perhaps fallen ill, that some relation had called on her, that she was impatiently waiting for me to come back.


The electric lamp was on. Jeanne was asleep on her back. Her watch, which she never put down on the marble table-top, was lying on a book.

So that she should know what time I had come

69

home, I woke her, though I hesitated over what part of her body I ought to touch.

Her look reassured me. She was so sleepy she could not guess what had been going on. I lowered my eyes like Jeanne when she is afraid her dress is too low-cut, or as I do when I am trying to see my nose. There was nothing unusual about me. Nevertheless I felt that my hands had the heat of a body warmer than mine, and that the outside air had scarcely chilled my jacket and that if I had taken it off my chest and arms would have been burning hot.

Jeanne spoke and, before I understood what she was saying, I realized that she did not know what I had been doing. She had gone to sleep without pins in her hair. She had not done up the neck of her nightgown for fear of being strangled in her sleep.

'Where have you been?'

Out of an inexplicable fear of being touched, I dared not reply that I had been for a walk.

'I have been at a café.'

She scrutinized me, scaring me when her eyes fell on my collar, which I cannot see even when I bow my head, with such a penetrating look that I should not have been surprised if she had guessed an address or a name.

'Armand, come here.'

I had a fit of dizziness. It seemed to me that everything was lost, that I had forgotten something in my pockets, that she would find out.

I sat down on the edge of the bed, by her feet, which were straight under the covers, the only part of her which did not follow the line of her body and which seemed to me as absurd as the position of toys when they have fallen down.

'You have been with a woman.'

This word made me blush. I should have blushed

70

even if I had not been with Marguerite, just as I blush when anyone mentions a theft near me. I smiled. I tried to be the same as when I was not blushing. By sheer will-power I managed to speak in a natural voice, so that Jeanne would have to think my face was flushed because of the heat.

'You have been with a woman.'

She was repeating what she had just said. It did not need any more for me to recover my confidence. Now she was annoying me. Only occasionally do I get angry. This time I could not restrain myself at being suspected without proof.

'You are getting on my nerves, Jeanne!'

'I know you have been with a woman.'

Then I began to speak harshly. Her face cleared. She was happy. My anger proved my innocence. She did not stir for fear that a movement might interrupt me. I was aware that she wanted me to continue in this tone for a long time.

But a moment later, seeing that my angry words made her so sure of my innocence filled me with remorse. I fell silent. She took my hand. Although she knew that I did not like her to kiss it, she put it to her lips.

8

The rain was so fine that it was necessary to look a long way ahead to make it out. I had rested my forehead against one of the window-panes of our bedroom. The drops running down the glass did not touch me.

It was midday. Jeanne had gone to sleep again. I kept trying to see her in the window in spite of the transparency of the glass.

Because of our bodies, all the soft furnishings and bed-clothes, the wallpaper, it was warm in the flat. I lit a cigarette. Instead of rising, the smoke, like mist, drifted to the bed, spreading itself against the mirror at the same time as its reflection. It was grey. The sky was grey. Everything I touched, especially iron, china and marble, was damp. Some women were crossing the courtyard. The bread they were carrying was wrapped in tissue paper, in spite of the rain.

I left the window. I looked at myself in the dressing-table mirror because it was bevelled.

I had not dressed. My face and hands were still as warm as my body. I thought of Marguerite, alone in her hotel room.

The city's clocks were chiming. I entertained myself by counting the strokes, hoping every time, I do not know why, that one of the strikers would go wrong and eleven or thirteen strokes ring out.

But nothing went wrong. Everything was following its normal course. So now we were settling into an afternoon which would pass slowly, divided by short hours until the evening, when the clocks would wake up at last.

I stood in the middle of the room. When I do not know what to do with myself I always stand in the middle of a room, so that I can be equally far from any occupation which might occur to me.

I had forgotten how many chairs there were in Marguerite's room. I tried to remember, as one tries to remember a forgotten detail in order to be able to sleep.

Jeanne coughed. I waited for a few moments. Then I went quietly up to the bed in order to surprise her. I leaned so far over her that I was almost brushing against her face, and, to rouse her, I pulled faces.

She opened her eyes.

Then I burst into laughter. She looked at me. Astonishment made her eyes look more lively than they usually did when she opened them. I was still laughing. It was because I was so tense. Laughing provided some relief. Tears came into the corners of my eyes. I wiped them away with the side of my hand, like a child.

At last I became calm. I was breathing hard. I did not reply to Jeanne's questions. So that she should not have to look up at me, I sat down on the bed.

She looked me straight in the eye. She liked doing that. She attached a lot of importance to holding a person's gaze. She knew the eye-colour of everyone who came near her. When she mentioned one of her friends, she talked of the girl who was shorter than she was, with grey-green or blue-black eyes.

She drew her legs from under the sheets, looked carefully at them one after the other, and twisted round, trying hard to see them from behind, as if she were being followed.

She asked me to bring her slippers and put them on for her. I got the feet the wrong way round because I was holding the left slipper in my left hand. She laughed, covered her legs with the end of the sheet just as she would have pulled down her dress so that I should not see her knees, assumed the pose of a woman taken by surprise and performed a few *entrechats*, without haste, pointing her toes to imitate a dancer.

She stopped and tried to kiss her ankle, because I could do that. It was beautifully shaped. Jeanne was proud of it. Like ugly women, she was proud of various small points, of her feet, her hair and her ears.

All these affectations were setting my nerves on edge. I stood up. She copied me, jumping on to the bedside rug and this time demonstrating how agile she was. As sometimes happened, that day she wanted to produce for me a kind of inventory of all her good points.

While she stood and powdered herself before the almost horizontal mirror of the dressing-table, I had gone back to the window. I rested my forehead against the glass, in the same place, because the spot was still warm, and looked out, with the damp curtain drawn in such a way that nothing but my face could be seen from opposite.

It was past midday. There was no longer anything to wait for. The rain was still falling. It trickled out of the flower-pots through the little holes at the bottom. On a window-sill was a bottle half-full of water in spite of the narrowness of the neck.

I could hear Jeanne coming and going. Suddenly she called me. I turned round. Naked in front of the wardrobe mirror so that she could see her raised arms, she had adopted the pose of a statue. Turning her head cautiously towards me, so that she did not break the line of her body, she asked.

'Do you like me like this?'

But when she was tired and wanted to lower her arms she asked me to close my eyes.

74

When we had had lunch, I went out. I was in a hurry to see Lucien again to complain about his behaviour, and above all to allay the fear which had not left me since the previous day.

It was still raining. The hats of passers-by, even though they were made of felt, were streaming with water. Because I remembered how water used to ruin my clockwork toys, I was for a moment surprised that the rain did no harm to the cars. I noticed that I had brought two handkerchiefs with me. I almost threw one of them away, because I so much dislike having anything useless with me.

Suddenly I felt a pain in the groin, a short, stabbing pain. I went on walking, full of anxiety, fearing that the same pain would come back, that it would swoop down on me later on, that it might be the symptom of some serious illness.

But nothing happened; it was over. I thought about it for a few more minutes, then, when I arrived at Lucien's house, I forgot it.


I was immediately struck by the unfriendliness of his expression when he caught sight of me. He did not ask me in. Without glancing at me or saying a word, he sat down again and looked at the book on the table.

I closed the door. He raised his head at the sound to see if I had come in or gone away. Then, turning a page as if he had finished reading it just as I had pushed the door to, he immersed himself in his reading.

I was going towards him to offer him my hand when he leapt to his feet and, as if I had been taller than he, he backed away.

If it had not been for the bulk of my clothing, he would have seen my heart beating. My lips were dry. If I had been suffering from some physical complaint I

75

could not have been more aware of it.

'What is the matter, Lucien?'

He was holding his book in his hand, trying hard in his nervousness to roll it up.

I searched my memory for what I could have done to offend him so. Was he still annoyed with me for having taken his sister's side? It was not possible. There was something else which as yet I hardly suspected.

Perhaps Marguerite had come there during the morning. She had spoken. She had told how I had been to see her in the evening and had kissed her. Then I reflected that her shyness would make such a thing impossible. That cheered me up so that I almost told her brother everything myself. I cannot keep a secret from a friend. Also I felt a certain pleasure in seeing Lucien behaving so offensively, because it would have been very difficult for me if he had been friendly at a time when I was hiding something from him.

'Why are you annoyed with me, Lucien?'

This time he looked into my eyes so insistently that I felt guilty of a much more serious fault than I had supposed.

He was pale. His empty hand was trembling. His face had no expression, either gentle or hard. It was the face of a man I no longer knew. Even his body, which could not change, in its familiar garments, seemed to me to belong to a stranger.

Then I was frightened. I was frightened of the objects in his pockets. I was frightened that he knew, that what I had done was more serious than I realized. It seemed to me that I was no longer master of my own life, that this man was in control of it. I waited anxiously for him to speak, because it would have made it so much easier for me to know what he held against me.

He was standing upright. He had thrown the book on to the table even though there were two glasses on it. For a moment he seemed humble, merely annoyed. I was becoming more confident when he again looked hostile.

I briefly wondered if I should speak first and tell him that I had kissed his sister, so that this confession might lessen my fault.

I saw Jeanne. In my memory she had no face. I saw only her hair, hands and breasts. She was asleep, with her arms and legs folded. Like that, she seemed to know nothing. She was calm. My life was about to be shattered. Once again I should be alone, as before, even more alone.

And Lucien's eyes never left me. He had one hand in the pocket of his trousers. He came up to me and wagged his finger at me.

'Brute!'

I trembled, I took a step backwards. My hands were numb as if I no longer had any fingers, as if they came to a point like branches.

'Aren't you ashamed, you brute?'

Although I was so pale, a sudden flush burned my cheeks. I looked straight at him. Nevertheless, I could still see the window and the table, all at the same time.

'You have a woman who is well off, who does everything for you and . . .'

His lips shaped every syllable. They sounded one after the other with immense clarity. An unexpected power was released with every movement. His collar was tight. Now and again I could see his teeth. They were held slightly apart as if they were about to bite.

I stammered out the first word that came into my head. It did not make sense, but still it was a word.

'Of course . . .'

Anything else I could have done seemed useless.

'You are happy and you try to lead a little girl astray. You go to her room in the evening, and you take advantage of the impression you have made on her. It is shameful. But you won't get away with it.'

He struck the table hard, hard enough to hurt himself so that the pain would make him still more violent.

'Go away, get out of here. Taking advantage of a child.'

He was silent for a moment and his face took on an expression of disgust.

'You think you only have to want something, don't you? Answer me, go on, answer. You took advantage of our situation. Anyone who behaves like you can well be generous. But it will not make you happy. You have to play fairer than that in life. Do you hear?'

Lucien no longer had any control over himself. His voice cracked. He went to and fro across the room, going near the furniture so that he could kick it, and sometimes missing.

My head was whirling. A single thought would not leave me. Would Jeanne hear about all this? I became humble.

'Lucien, listen.'

'Shut up!'

'Listen . . . I'm sorry . . . You don't know what happened.'

'I do know; Marguerite told me.'

'It was a moment of weakness. It could have happened to you, Lucien . . . I swear I shall never see her again.'

I spoke without knowing what I was saying, trying to calm him down more by the sound of my voice than by the sense of my words.

'Forgive me, Lucien. Afterwards we shall get back to what we were before. Your sister is very nice, but, as you said, she is not for me.'

A gust of rain struck the zinc roofs as if a tree laden with fruit had been shaken. The sky grew light. A row of drops quivered on the railing at the window.

Lucien, with his mouth shut and his eyes half-closed, must be thinking about all the harsh words he had just uttered. I thought I could make out, from his weary expression, that he was sorry he had become so angry.

I kept quiet, fearing that any word might drive away his dawning calm. After the scene that had just taken place, the silence was awkward only for me. Lucien was pursuing thoughts which, at the slightest provocation, would throw him into a passion again. I tried to follow them with him. I imagined he was thinking about his sister, then, because he looked at me, about me. I made myself small and humble, so that nothing should release a new outburst of rage.

I wanted to speak. I watched for a suitable moment, as if we had to speak at the same time. He closed his eyes for a second.

'Lucien, I swear . . . I shall not see her again.'

These few words did not deflect the train of his thoughts. He remained deep in meditation where, this time, I could not follow him, as I did not know what had set it off.

For the first time since our exchange he thought about himself, bit his lips and stroked his hair.

'Lucien.'

'What?'

'Are you still angry with me?'

A light gleamed in one of his eyes, the one that was nearer the window. His nostrils flared as if he was trying hard to catch some scent. Just as some people are capable of controlling their ears or certain muscles in their arms or legs, he was able to control his nostrils.

I had spoken too soon. He was not ready for a

reconciliation. A new fear swept over me. Was he going to begin again? Was he going to threaten to hit me, to start reviling me once more?

It was as if I had just let go of him. I did not yet know which way he would fall. Then he released his hands. He raised his eyes. I was saved.

As if somebody had been having a bath in the room, the window-panes were steamed up. I restrained myself from rushing to him and shaking him warmly by the hand. Although I was inwardly bursting with joy, I took care to appear unmoved.

Only then did I notice that the stove was alight. For the first time I heard a bus going by in a neighbouring street.

I walked confidently to the door. Before opening it I turned round. After a moment's silence, with my head high, I said in a clear voice:

'Goodbye, Lucien.'


The rain had stopped. Drops were still running down the houses, but they were no longer coming from the sky. People on foot were walking easily in the middle of the pavements. Between two clouds which the wind was blowing along at the same pace there was a patch of sky, fresh and blue.

Now I was sorry I had left so hastily. It worried me that I no longer knew what Lucien was thinking. I was afraid that in my absence he would grow angry again and go and tell Jeanne everything.

Remembering how he had been before I left him, I became confident again. He would never dare go to my house, even if, for a moment, at the height of his anger, he had considered doing so.

I sat in a café to wait until it was time for dinner. In

spite of everything, I was too upset to see Jeanne again then. Deep down I was afraid of being in her presence. When I am upset I am no good at hiding it. She would have questioned me. It would be better to spend the rest of the afternoon alone, thinking.

9

When I went in, Jeanne was sitting in the drawing-room, like a visitor, surrounded by none of the objects with which she might have been expected to fill a free hour. It just used to annoy me when she sat like that, because in her it was a sign of lassitude such as I cannot bear around me. This time, seeing her unoccupied made me fearful.

The draught moving from one room to the other, the lights from the house opposite which I could see through the windows, increased my worry.

The doors and shutters were open. That Jeanne, who was usually so careful of her comfort, should not have closed them to make the room cosier and prevent the heat escaping astonished me.

When I came in she was in the habit of kissing me, smelling my breath (she used to be confused about the smells) so she could scold me if I had been drinking, touching my face under the eyes where no one but she could do it, putting her hands caressingly into the most open of my pockets, sliding two fingers into it, as if I had been laden with parcels, to extract my small change and doing it clumsily because women do not know how to put their fingers into a pocket.

That evening she did not stir.

I dared not go near her. It was eight o'clock. I had left Lucien at the end of the afternoon. It dawned on me that he could have come there in the interval and told her everything.

I lost my head. I was gasping and could only breathe through my mouth. Through the thickness of my soles, I felt as if I was holding myself poised.

Jeanne had kept her gloves near her. Her hat, which she usually put away before anything else, was on the table, at the edge, because it had rolled a little way before coming to a halt. She was wearing a long jacket, as if she was going out. The fur collar hid her neck and chin. She had fastened it as she did when she used to bow her head and smile to look like a photograph.

Without saying a word, I went into the dining-room. There, when it was not a meal-time, I felt safe. The stove was out but its porcelain handles were still warm. A sugar-basin reminded me of dessert and made me notice that the table had not been laid.

So that no noise should penetrate the wall which divided me from the drawing room, I opened the door of the sideboard which did not squeak. No fresh cut had been made in the left-over food. Jeanne had not had dinner.

I went back into the bedroom, afraid I should find the mirror-fronted wardrobe locked. Its door was half open. For a moment I felt more cheerful. But it was not long before fear swept over me again.

The letters were no longer on the mantelpiece.

Jeanne had hidden them. She knew. She did not want me to share her life any longer. In order to comfort herself, she had read them again.

I sat down, not because I was tired, but hoping that, as in physical discomfort, a change of position would bring relief. It did not. I had palpitations. I could feel them all over my chest, a very little stronger on the left, climbing up towards my throat and neck as I then became breathless.

A light-bulb on the wall lit up the bed. One day, when I was away, Jeanne had put some pale fabric around it. I had been troubled when I got back. I stood up. I could remember our first words in that light.

How cold it was now on the bedspread, without those letters!

With determination I began to look for them. I felt that my happiness depended on them. I picked up the pillows and raised the mattress, where Jeanne might have slipped them, thinking that as I knew she had things there, it would not occur to me to look there. Then, trembling, I re-made the bed carefully so that she should not notice anything, but however I arranged the bedspread there were still new creases in it.

The drawers were closed even though Jeanne usually left two or three open because of her wish to appear absent-minded and rather disorganized.

The letters were in one of them.

A deep contentment flooded me. My heart went on beating as before, but without distressing me. I drew breath. Lucien had not come. He had not told her anything. He was incapable of doing anything so mean. I had been mistaken about him and Jeanne. The world was a better place than I had thought. I had been beginning to believe that I was being persecuted, to see signs of a plot in the smallest object which had been moved from its place. A morbid fear of everything about me had been warping my judgement, turning one of Lucien's gestures into a fit of rage and Jeanne's slight weariness into schemes against me.

I made a sound. Like a child, to test its bounciness, I sat on the bed although I had just made it carefully, then, confidently, I returned to the drawing-room.

By a trick of the way the mirrors were arranged, the room seemed shaped like a short gallery illuminated at three points by the lights of the same chandelier. But the fireplace in the mirror of which the room was reflected, spoiled the illusion of size.

Jeanne was sitting in the same place.

Her fingers had moved. Because they were hanging lower as the tips of branches do in the evening, she looked tired.

The fear to which I was disposed began to over-whelm me again. Everywhere I noticed unaccustomed details. The chairs were too far apart for anyone to have touched them.

I walked round the room as if I was looking for something, in order to provide an excuse for my comings and goings in the flat.

At last I sat down opposite Jeanne.

Not to speak amounted to a confession. Never-theless I dared not say a word. She lowered her eyes. One of her fingers moved, then went back to its place between the other fingers.

From her breathing, her hands, her face, even her clothes, I tried to guess what she was thinking about. I could not. That her whole being should be before me, without a single detail giving away what she was thinking, annoyed me.

Gently, as if I had been hit to punish me for for-getting something, I cursed myself for a fool.

I was deeply regretting my lack of intuition when it occurred to me to wonder what I would have done if it had been Jeanne who had deceived me. I would have been careful not to tell her immediately that I knew. Like her, I would have waited as long as possible.

This observation devastated me. I tried to find some comfort from the difference in our characters. Jeanne was much more quick-tempered than I. If she had known anything she would not have been able to hide it from me. But this theory, instead of cheering me, was so uncertain that it left me crushed.

Jeanne still did not move. I realized that this stillness, which was at last coming to seem natural, was the sign of great unhappiness. Something had happened in my absence. I was lost. I wanted to see Lucien again immediately and ask him if he had come. I was angry that I had not, before I left him, asked him a question that would have reassured me now. I had my doubts about the calm that had followed his anger. He was spiteful. He had said that I would not get away with it.

I was worn out. Everything around me was cold and distant. I stood up, intending to go back into our room, to go to bed, to pretend to sleep so that I should not learn anything that evening.

I went out silently, exaggerating my movements in order to make no noise. In the hall I switched on the light.

Suddenly, as I stood in the dim light of the passage, still hesitating whether to take another step, I heard Jeanne's voice.

'Armand, I must speak to you.'

Up until that moment I had been afraid of one thing only, that Lucien had told her that I had kissed Marguerite. Now I was frightened of being punished. In that instant I realized that she had rights over me, that she could take her revenge, and the world would think she was in the right.

I went back into the drawing-room, but not before I had switched off the hall light, as I was careful to remain myself.

Standing up, facing me, completely altered, Jeanne examined me from head to foot, not daring to be contemptuous for fear that it would have emphasized her height. I realized that I was a stranger to her, that nothing there belonged to me any more. Various objects I owned passed before my eyes. It seemed to me that I was being pushed out, that I had not time to collect them.

Although I drew near to her as I walked, she seemed always to be the same height, far away, with her back to the window.

I waited for her to explain herself. She looked me in the eye. She half opened her mouth before she produced a word so that the effort of moving her lips would not increase the effort of speaking.

'Is what Lucien told me true?'

I did not reply. Perhaps she was referring to something else.

'Answer me.'

I dared look her straight in the eyes, first one then the other, without being able to keep my gaze still.

There was a mahogany table between us. Aimless thoughts kept passing through my mind. I saw Jeanne's reflection in the table, clearer than mine in a rectangle without dust where a book had been. I saw the iron fire-guard with one side missing, the felt of the card-table, which was coming unglued at the place where it folded, the pedals of the piano, the screw of the piano-stool, the door-stops which protected the wood-work, the carpet beneath which the parquet was not polished.

Jeanne went on speaking and now I saw only her, only her face in the minutest detail. Her thin set lips and fixed gaze gave her an expression I did not recognize, so new to me that it was as if, for the first time, we had happened to be together in the presence of a corpse. Under one of her eyes was a mark which grew red after meals. I had the same sort of mark at the base of my nose. They were doubtless both caused by a broken vein under the skin. It was one of the things we had in common which made us like each other.

Because she had been holding her head in her hands, she had released her ears from the hair which hid them. As they were a deeper colour, they looked healthier than her pale face.

She grimaced. Her lower lip covered the other one.

Her eye-lashes stuck together, as if she had been crying. The flesh at the corners of her eyes was twitching. A fortyish wrinkle, starting from her cheeks passed under her chin.

'Armand, what you did is not right. I trusted you. I thought you loved me a little. It is not right . . . You do not know how I have suffered since I was told everything.'

As she spoke she fixed her gaze on my eyes, exaggerating its steadiness so that I should understand that she wanted to read my mind. As if I had been face to face with a medium, I thought about some piece of stupidity impossible to guess at.

'I know what you are thinking. You are saying to yourself: "How boring this woman is." I can see it in your eyes. Well, that will not stop me talking to you as you deserve . . . Do you hear, Armand?'

She broke off to wait for a reply. I dared not half open my lips, nor breathe audibly, nor even make a movement for fear that, thinking I was about to speak, silence would cause too much disillusion. I was pale. I made myself look at her as I listened, making especially sure that I did not lower my eyes. I was always the first to turn my head away, otherwise I would have blinked my eyes and she would have thought I was making fun of her.

Luckily the clock only struck the half hour. Too long a sound would have forced us to listen to it together. In spite of myself I looked at the clock. An hour had passed without my noticing. It was as if the hands had jumped over the space which that hour took up on the dial.

Suddenly, Jeanne went out in the direction of the bedroom, without turning round, with the haste of a woman who is about to cry.

I remained alone in the drawing-room where the

chandelier and chairs were meant for several people. I sat down in Jeanne's armchair, because it had no piece of furniture or wall behind it, because I like to be able to lean back when I cross my legs.

That no one understood me plunged me into great sadness. I had done no harm. It was not deceiving a woman to kiss a poor child who was alone in the world. However I did not feel strong enough to convince Jeanne of that.

It seemed to me that nothing which would exonerate me would change her opinion in the least. Because I had been suspected and despised I no longer believed I could defend myself with words. Objections were jumbled in my mind, just as logical and just as deep as the excuses for what I had done.

Only the immediate opportunity of doing something decisive could save me.

I wanted to withdraw into myself and find the energy to enjoy life again.

Up until then, every time I had been unhappy, I had found comfort in the injustice. Time seemed to me to be divided equally between good and evil. But I had worn out too much of that feeling to be a victim of it. It had become blunt. It was useless for me to exaggerate the injustice from which I was suffering, I remained crushed, with not even the smallest hope born of pain to give me courage. Humility was no more fruitful. People were right to despise me. I was not worthy of being loved or helped. For the first time in my life, I had the feeling that no one on earth would deign to have pity on me.

I closed my eyes, hoping that in the dark I would change, that my distress was only temporary. But my eyes were open behind my lids. The faint yellow light passing through them reminded me that the chandelier was still on. Activated by the same sort of feeling that made me bite biscuits in a way that left the semi-circular mark of my teeth in them, I clenched my hands violently so that my nails should leave an imprint on my flesh.

I opened my eyes. The drawing-room lights had the same rays of the same length. On the furniture the same reflections had not moved. I had the feeling that the light was as independent of me as the daylight was, that the switch was not in the room or in the house, that if I had wanted to turn off the light I should not have been able to. The doors were closed. Through the fireplace, which was closer to her bedroom than the walls, I could hear Jeanne undressing. Noises too were the same, as if nothing had happened.

Then I heard her going to bed. I did not know if she had switched the light off. Although this was of no importance in itself, I got up and approached the bed-room door in such a way that my shadow covered it, so that the edges of the door-jamb, if they were light, would show up more clearly.

They were dark. She had turned off the light.

Then I became aware, more than at the time when she had been speaking to me, how far apart from each other we now were. In spite of what I had done, the light disturbed her when she was trying to sleep. Already she had taken the decision to remain on her own, even though we were both there.

I sat down again.

It was only a long while later, when I thought she would be asleep, that I went into the bedroom.

10

I undressed noiselessly so that Jeanne, even if she were awake, would not hear me.

The shutters had not been pulled to. I put my shoes on the carpet, toe first. I placed my clothes on a chair, cautiously, so that their weight should not make it rock, taking care that nothing fell out of my pockets and that no buttons, which among so much cloth might be in unexpected places, knocked against the back.

Suddenly, weary of being quiet and because it would relieve my feelings without making any noise, I threw my socks haphazardly in front of me.

Dragging my feet so that I would push aside rather than crush anything lying on the floor, I went warily towards Jeanne, with my eyes lowered so she would not see the light from them, walking with one hand spread out before me in order that, if a door happened to be open, I should be aware of it.

I slid my fingers slowly along the woodwork of the bed, as if along a banister, slowly, in order not to graze them on the carving at the corners.

By the bedside table which wobbles because it always has one leg on the rug, I stopped. Every evening I put my collar-stud on that table. Because of this habit, small like itself, I was holding it in my hand, without thinking.

Jeanne was stretched out along the wall. I hesitated to slip between the sheets for fear my joints might creak.

At last I bent forward, lifted one leg in such a way

that the weight of my body remained on the ground until the very last moment, balancing easily because the foot I was standing on was bare.

When I was half lying down, I picked up the other leg, stretching it out beforehand so that I did not have to do it in bed. Then I pushed my feet under the covers because I cannot sleep when they are outside the bed.

I was in bed. Jeanne, if she was asleep, had heard nothing.

I like walking and moving silently. In the preceding months I had often amused myself by going up to Jeanne on tiptoe, so she did not realize it, to give her a fright.

The room was dark. As I listened to Jeanne, I realized that she was awake. I could hear, with only one ear, because I was lying on the other, her eyes opening and closing and the sound of her breathing. From the noise her tongue made I could tell whether her mouth was open or closed. Although I was so used to those scarcely perceptible sounds, it seemed to me that she was getting up, that she was about to go away, when all she did was move.

Gradually my eyes became accustomed to the dark. I could see the sheet which she had drawn up over her shoulder, but which the air could get underneath all the same. I could see her hair which spread over on to my pillow, without her being aware of it, like a child at the seaside, when its mother is sewing.

She sighed, although I had not heard her take a breath beforehand. Savage as I had been when she had spoken to me harshly, I felt myself becoming gentle now that she was suffering silently.

The bedclothes had fallen down again between our two bodies. She was holding herself quite straight, on her side, with her nightgown pulled down to her knees, fearing even the scarcely perceptible contact of our feet.

I heard her slide her hand under the pillow. Suddenly she hid her face. She must be crying.

I could find no word to comfort her. She was crying without moving. I was so touched that I wanted to clasp her against me and kiss her. But she had not yet slept. The thoughts going through her mind at that moment were bound up with the earlier ones. I decided to wait until she was calmer and surprise her when she woke up with her spirit refreshed.

I did not know whether time was passing quickly or slowly. Although I had closed my eyes, I was as wide awake as if they had been open. I should have liked to doze as I did during nights on guard, enough to dream, not too much to be able to get up at the slightest noise.

Because I felt dizzy when I was not thinking, I tried very hard to pursue my memories, the first that came into my head. When I had finished, I opened my eyes. There I was, all small in the long, high room, far, very far from the window which was scarcely lighter than the walls.

In order to avoid stretching my hand in the air where it might have met Jeanne's, I slid it towards the edge of the mattress as far as the cold solid bar of the metal frame, the touch of which revived me.

For a long time I passed from one memory to another. Then, quietly, as when I am talking to myself, I called:

'Jeanne.'

She did not reply.

'Jeanne,' I said again, without raising my voice, for she could certainly hear me.

That name, flying from my pillow to hers, united us. It re-echoed in the darkness after it had been spoken. I could feel it in my mouth as if my tongue had kept the shape it had taken in order to utter its last syllable. It obliterated every other thought.

Nevertheless, no movement, no word greeted it.

The silence and the night hummed in my ears. I waited a moment then, as quietly as before, I murmured once again:

'Jeanne!'

This time she stirred, but it was to cover herself up better, as if I had merely aroused her instinct in her.

I could not contain myself any longer.

'Forgive me, Jeanne, I did not know it was so serious. I am sorry.'

To start off with my voice trembled. But talking like that, without gestures, to Jeanne who had her back to me made my words lose their sincerity even as I spoke them.

I continued nevertheless.

'Please, Jeanne, forget it all. You know quite well I could not do anything wrong.'

She lifted her head, which, for a second, because she was lying down and had her arms at her sides seemed grotesque because of the memory of people who move when they are pretending to be dead.

'I am not listening to you, Armand.'

Those words chilled me. Even though I knew that people cannot control their hearing, that if I had spoken, she would have heard my voice even against her will, I was silent.

Everything was over. My happiness no longer depended on myself. Great anguish flooded over me. I could not be gentler or more tender than I had just shown myself to be.

I was going to cry. My saliva flowed freely. My eyes grew moist. Because I was lying down, because the skin of the temples is more sensitive than the skin of the cheeks, my tears seemed more copious than when I weep in an upright position.

I did not want Jeanne to hear me. I wept silently, shifting every time part of the pillow grew damp.

I had no more strength. Numbness overwhelmed me, interrupted several times when I started because, before I go to sleep, I always dream that I am tripping over a stone.

I began to feel comfortable. Everything was all right. I relaxed. I could go to sleep if I wanted to.

In the middle of the night I opened my eyes as easily as if I had not been asleep. It was perhaps two o'clock in the morning. The tears had dried on my cheeks. It seemed to me that my eyes had grown larger. There they were, blue and open wide, in the middle of my face.

I heard a distant clock striking. It was the time of night when it is impossible to tell what time it is by the chimes of the clocks, because the hours, the half-hours and the quarters become muddled.

Jeanne was no doubt asleep. I could hear her regular breathing. This time around us was real night when the smallest of lights is not a continuation of the day and has been put out at least once, when clothes are black, heavy and forgotten.

In a burst of tenderness, I moved close to Jeanne, searched for her mouth and kissed her slowly. Her lips parted, she let herself go. She had forgotten. We loved each other as we had before. She was forgiving me when, suddenly, remembering everything, she pushed me away.

Although the day is divided into so many instants it was exactly at seven o'clock that I woke up.

It was not yet broad daylight. Jeanne was asleep. Her

95

body moved with a regular motion which could be seen at her shoulder. I remembered everything and immediately I experienced a heaviness against which, as I lay motionless, I had no defence.

A long day was beginning for me alone. It was very close to the day before. My sleep had been too short for me to have changed. I had been resting for three hours, counting the time it took me to go to sleep.

I am usually full of confidence in the morning, but now I was as much at a loss as in the middle of the night. I dared not stir, although when I wake up early, I turn over so that the feeling that I have just gone to bed helps me to go to sleep again.

I felt that as soon as Jeanne opened her eyes something decisive would happen. Her head had slipped from the pillow which, on its own, seemed part of an empty bed. Like that, in that rather graceful position, it was as if she still loved me, as if nothing had happened, as if she would wake up smiling, as if the words she had uttered lacked importance beside the reality of her giving herself up to me.

The morning light reached the suggestive prints high on the walls which we used to look at in the evening. Everything seemed strange. Chairs which could be moved seemed as immovable as the wardrobe. My shoes on the floor looked at me like a tramp's in a ditch. Objects which I did not recognize puzzled me. From the fresh colour of the window-panes I realized that the sky was blue, that it would remain blue all day long, that the sun had already risen, and from the horizon was shedding a golden light on buildings facing east.

Now Jeanne was facing me. Her hands, mouth and eyes were closed. From time to time, to assist her breathing, she sniffed the air like a scent. Her paper-thin eyelids were criss-crossed with blue veins, as if the eyes had been too big for them.

My breath caressed her face. I turned my head aside so that it should not wake her.

Now and again she breathed more quickly as if she was about to wake up, or else she seemed to be swallowing something. Then I was afraid she would open her eyes, because I have always believed one cannot control one's throat when one is asleep.

Without a single warning movement her eyelids opened suddenly. Two eyes looked at me. Their pupils, like a cat's, were larger because it was still dark. They did not move. It was as if the eyes still covered them. Because those eyes were still, it seemed to me that they could only make out things that were motionless, that my movements escaped them.

Then I considered taking Jeanne in my arms. She had slept. In the morning perhaps my fault would seem less serious.

As I had in the night, I first murmured:

'Jeanne!'

She half-opened her mouth so that I should understand she was not answering because she did not want to.

I went on:

'Are you still angry with me?'

She leaned on her elbow in the middle of the pillow and looked behind her arm, twisting her flesh:

'No Armand. Why should I be angry with you? It is over between us.'

These words, because they were the first Jeanne spoke, seemed to me the exact reflection of her thoughts. I realized that she had taken a decision before going to sleep and that, since the hours of sleep had not weakened it, there was no longer anything to hope for. On the contrary, the more time passed, the further she would be from me. I was alone. It was irreparable and so much so that no emotion swept over me. I was calm. She was sitting on the bed. Although she must have been upset, she stretched out her arms as if to try to touch her toes without bending her legs.

Then, turning suddenly towards me, she asked me to get up so that she would not have to climb over me to get out of bed. I obeyed. I offered her my hand as I do when she is going down steps. She took it, gripped it hard, but let go of it immediately, as soon as she had put a foot on the ground.

I lay down again in the middle of the sheets, between our two warm places. I pulled down the sleeves of my nightshirt because I am cold when my arms are bare.

With the back of my neck resting against a pillow, I watched her getting dressed. She did not speak, even when she spent a minute looking for one of her stockings, even when she dropped her dress. She passed from one room to another, without hesitating, leaving the doors open when she was coming back.

When she was ready, she went into the drawing-room. I could not hear her any more.

11

I got up and walked on my heels to my slippers which, for once, she had not placed side by side.

My clothes were hanging over chairs which were half empty since Jeanne had got dressed. Making even less noise than when I had taken them off the day before, because the keys and small change had fallen to the bottom of the pockets, I put them on one by one, in the usual order.

That morning they were permeated with ordinary life. I scarcely touched them as I held them with the tips of my fingers. Unfolding them without Jeanne beside me reminded me of my former loneliness. The buttons, lining and seams missed her, as did everything which is independent of the cut.

I pulled back the sheets to air the bed. I put the pillows at the foot as I do when I sleep during the day.

I was ready in my turn. Although I had only just got up, I was yawning. Through the wall on which we used to knock three times to call each other, now that I was standing up, I could make out the rustle of a newspaper which, in my anxiety, I confused with the feebler rustle of a letter.

I dared not go into the drawing-room where there was no untidiness, no water, no cloth, nothing resembling tears, nothing which would have concealed them by soaking them up, where it was lighter, where I should have shown up more clearly.

At last I decided to push open the door. I took one step forward, then another.

In the middle of the room, Jeanne was sitting in one

of the armchairs which are usually placed against the walls.

I began to walk round in circles. Sometimes I stopped and turned round, without thinking about it, for fear of becoming dizzy. When I passed behind her, I could see the reverse side of the chair-back, covered with some fabric I had never noticed before.

That I should notice an unfamiliar detail at such a serious moment terrified me. Perhaps others would follow until they were so numerous that they would change my life.

The only sound I was then aware of was made by my own footsteps, louder when my right foot, which like my right arm is stronger, touched the floor.

Was Jeanne reading the newspaper she had in her hands? Was she thinking? Was she waiting for an opportunity to speak to me?

I stopped by the window. As I raised my head and counted the storeys of the building opposite ours, after reminding myself that we lived on the third floor, I noticed a ray of sun turning the slope of the roofs golden, a bit of the same night sky which had not had the time to change during my short sleep.

I turned round. A shawl was lying over the piano in such a way that one of the corners hung down to the floor.

Suddenly Jeanne stood up.

In that room where normally we could come and go by three ways, we found ourselves motionless, face to face.

'Armand!'

I looked at her. She was calm. She was avoiding my eyes. She hesitated for a second, just long enough to look me up and down then said:

'It would be better for us to part.'

I remained unmoved. These words, instead of

devastating me, produced a feeling of deep relief. It was the worst thing that could have happened to me and yet I remained the same. Nothing had changed since she had spoken. As I do during a fall in a dream, I let myself go, waiting for the impact which I could feel was still some way off.

I had often wondered if mental pain was preferable to physical suffering. It seemed to me that it was not, until the time when I became fully aware of my own distress.

'Yes, Armand, it is the right thing to do. I have thought about it for a long time. You are a child. I am older than you. I realize you cannot love a woman like me.'

Jeanne was tired. She was speaking in order to obey an order she had given herself several hours before. The gentleness in her voice softened the harshness of her words.

'You must go, Armand!'

The emotion I felt was so violent that I could not stop myself thinking that it was cutting my life short by some weeks. I was thrown back on myself. No one would comfort me. I was about to find myself alone, as I had been in the past.

With my hands outstretched, I went up to Jeanne. She watched me coming without drawing back.

'Jeanne!'

'What is the matter?'

I could not utter another word. A single tear rolled from one of my eyes, as if caused by the cold. My ears were burning. They could make out nothing, although I could see Jeanne's lips moving. My fingers were trembling, especially the little one, because it is weaker.

The doors were open. Our bedroom door, which had been used more than the others, would have closed at the least breath of air. The curtains had not been pulled right back. Jeanne had stopped as soon as a little light had made its way into the room.

She was standing very straight in the middle of the room. She was weaker than I. Even had I wanted her to, she certainly could not have turned me out without calling the neighbours. Her cheeks were white, her mouth so pale that the lipstick she had put on stained it instead of beautifying it. The furniture, although it was in its usual place, seemed further apart.

I was very close to her. If I had taken another step I should have touched her body.

To see her unmoved when I could have clasped her against me without stirring overwhelmed me.

I let myself fall on my knees at her feet. I raised my eyes and begged for pity. Because her left hand was near me, I seized hold of it. It was hotter than usual. But its warmth, like that of a strange hand, already no longer worried me, did not make me question my friend about her health.

Jeanne bowed her head. With her other hand she gently stroked my hair, so that it should not stand on end as it did when I entertained myself by playing the clown, so that everything we had done together should remain no more than a memory.

'Jeanne, forgive me!'

She avoided touching my head, playing only with my hair as if it simply belonged to me without forming part of me.

'I have nothing to forgive you for, my Armand. You have done nothing wrong. You were both young. What happened was inevitable. I ought to have suspected it, but I trusted you, you see.'

I released her hand which fell back beside her body. In spite of that she went on looking at me with the same pity.

I was hoping for the impossible. Perhaps she was about to burst into tears and to tell me to stay!

Oh! If she had said that, I do not know what I should have done for happiness. I should have thrown myself at her feet, broken vases and chair-stretchers, cried aloud. Then I should suddenly have fallen silent, because I am always afraid that my transports may last too long. It may mean having to control myself before the people with whom I am conversing or having to appear curt to them, but I never take long to recover my composure.

I was waiting, with a stitch in my side because of my emotion, the same sort of stitch I had had as a child when I ran and as a young man when I walked quickly. I tried to hide my panting by keeping my mouth half-open.

'Armand, you must go, now.'

It seemed to me that as she spoke those words she weakened, that she no longer had the strength to part from me. As if it had been a matter of pleasing an employer, I felt that if I were able to stay with her for another hour, she would forgive me. I wanted to speak.

'Come on, Armand, be reasonable.'

I tried to gain time. But, in her gentleness, she seemed to me to have made up her mind. I had been mistaken. In one hour, without raising her voice, she would ask me to leave her.

Then I realized that everything was over. I suddenly felt the same sense of desolation as after the death of a friend.

I touched the table with the tips of my fingers. The contact stopped me from thinking. I was far away from Jeanne. Memories were born, one by one, in my mind.

I saw myself as a child again, with my nails too short

for my parents to be able to cut them and my fair hair, a lock of which I still had; then as a small boy, born a few years before 1900, enjoying exhibitions and national festivals, who was sad to think he would die before the celebrations of the year 2000, who was afraid that his mother might mistake hemlock for chervil, who never laughed behind the back of teachers wearing glasses, who liked engines with wind-shields, who when he was reading hunted for descriptions of torture, as he did love-scenes later on, who especially liked history and geography, who had friends who now appeared to me, some full face. Others, the successful ones, in profile.

I saw again the books whose bindings I used to break in order to have a studious air, my father who, without his beard, would have had no chin, my mother's jewels and the small arms for toy soldiers that I used to sell, my young brother whom I never hit in the back.

I saw myself as a soldier who would rather lose an arm than a leg, two arms than a nose, two arms and a leg than the eyes, who was afraid that grenades might explode before the regulation number of seconds had elapsed, who never aimed at anyone for a joke, who had a friend who never refused him a cigarette until after he had had three, who had another friend born the same day, the same year, and who, like him, did not know the time or the address.

That past, which Jeanne knew about, about which she had often asked me to tell her, in which she had seemed interested, no longer moved her.

Everything was over. I thought of telling her that I had weak lungs, that I had always concealed from her that I supported an impoverished mother on my pocket-money, of telling her no matter what, and of telling her in tears, of admitting to a great mixture of deeds both glorious and despicable, even though I had not done one of them, so that astonishment should draw her attention to another side of me.

But I realized that would be useless too.

I took a step. It was the first time since she had got up that I had turned my back on her, as simply as after an everyday goodbye. My shadow did not turn with me. I remained alone before the half-open door of the hall where coats were hanging at more than a man's height.

I took another step, shorter than the earlier one, calculated like one before a step up or down. Everything in front of me still remained wretched.

I could not go on. I turned round and went back to the middle of the room, stopping before the sunlight gilding the walls, as if at such a moment I ought to refuse its light.

Jeanne had not stirred. She was looking at the place where I ought to have been.

'So you are turning me out, Jeanne?'

She rested her gaze on the parts of my face which showed my emotions most clearly, on my eyes, nostrils and lips.

'No, Armand. I am asking you to go.'

I suddenly noticed that neither of us had spoken without using the other's Christian name. At the moment of parting, the names took on a new significance. They were the only part of the being we were leaving that remained to us.

I was resigned. There are moments which no word, no regret, no despairing act can touch, when one remains as powerless before a human being as before an object.

I looked at her. I was about to leave this woman before me for ever. Her body was already taking on the look it had had before it belonged to me. Its faults, although I often thought about them, were disappearing. It seemed as perfect as the bodies of women who are strangers to me.

I drew away backwards. In the hall I stopped for the last time. She had followed me with her eyes. There was no piece of furniture between us. I had not gone down any steps. We were still standing on the same level.

I stretched a hand towards her, the longer, the right one. She turned away her head to indicate her refusal. Everything about her was perfectly clear. Even with my eyes closed I could have gone up to her and kissed her right on the mouth.

As when one wakes up in the morning, even the hangings were not moving. I could already make out a noise on the staircase. A neighbour was going up to his flat. He could think. He was calm.

Then I could see and hear no more. Because words were still left to me, I murmured:

'Goodbye, Jeanne.'

12

I came out and turned right, for no reason, merely because when I am left to myself I always turn right, as I do in a wood.

White clouds, so small that their whole shadow could follow the streets, were now crossing the sky without touching one another.

It was Sunday. I should have been unaware of it if the silent houses, the children wearing new hats with the brims turned up or down in the way they did not like, the clear water flowing along beside the pavements, had not informed me of it.

It was early. Nevertheless the clocks went on striking for a long time, as at midday, giving a misleading idea of what time it was, with the solemnity of a cannon thundering out for some celebration.

I began to go along an avenue. Without my suspecting it, it led to the district where I had lived when I had been poor and alone.

The houses were becoming familiar. A porch reminded me of a storm. From that moment on, I tried very hard to revive the memories that avenue evoked by walking slowly, so that they could come to mind before I had overtaken them.

In front of this confectioner's I had stopped during the New Year celebrations, because of a crib they had. This was the bench I had sat on one evening, boldly, with my legs inwards, in order to lean on the back. I had hung around this newspaper kiosk, being afraid every time that it might be closed. From this window a woman had looked at me one spring evening when the downy fluff from the buds was floating in the air.

I lit a cigarette, so clumsily that the flame scorched it half way up. I was not hungry. Nevertheless I was aware of a hollow in my stomach which I was careful not to make bigger by swallowing saliva.

Because I had scarcely slept, my hands were dry and grey, as they are after a journey, my nails covered with white skin which I do not like looking at closely.

I thought about Jeanne, trying to guess what she was doing then. The idea of going back to her flat, of begging her again to keep me, occurred to me briefly. Perhaps she was sorry she had turned me out. Like everyone else, I often incline to the belief that people feel sorry when they have made someone suffer.

I should have liked to watch her, hidden in a doorway, not on the side where the bell was so that I did not get in anyone's way, and wait for her for hours, every day, follow her on the opposite pavement, leave bunches of flowers without labels with her concierge, and presents that did not have string with the name of the shop on it so that she should not be disappointed, and letters with stamps, so that she should think they had come by post and the postman had forgotten to cancel them.

I should have arranged for her to see me in the distance. She would have pretended not to recognize me. After a month she would have been moved. One day she would have come up to me, forgiven me and asked me to go back to her flat. And she would have put my belongings back in the places where they had been before I went so that any marks I might have left would be in the same places.

I stopped for a moment in front of a private house where, one afternoon, as I passed by with Jeanne, I had pretended to have been born.

A clock showing quarter to twelve reminded me of

the evenings when the two of us were going home from the cinema. Because I was not carrying anything, was dressed as usual and because, when I went out in the morning, I used not to go back until one o'clock so that lunch was ready, I still did not realize what had happened.

Perhaps because of a young woman who looked at me, because of my motionlessness which nothing disturbed, suddenly, in a busy street, I became fully aware that everything was over, that I was penniless, as alone as somebody faced with a serious illness.

My breath failed, as it does in a dream when I wrestle with a man stronger than myself. My head spun. I set off again without knowing whether I was walking straight, with the impression that behind me my footsteps indicated to everyone the uncertainty of my gait.

There was no wind. It was less cold. It did not take me long to recover. I reckoned it was twenty-one hours since I had eaten, twenty-six since I had had a cup of coffee.

The idea of going to see Marguerite or Lucien occurred to me, but I did not feel brave enough to get angry or make a scene.

Now I found myself in the middle of the district where I had lived so wretchedly.

I had not gone back there since I had got to know Jeanne so that the pleasure of seeing it again might be increased and also because of an unconscious fear of what had just happened, in order that, when I was alone once again, I might have the joy of immersing myself in unspoilt memories.

I passed by a hotel where I had, as always, occupied a room with a number between thirty and forty; a bar where I used to drink my coffee out of a cup with a metal handle which replaced the broken one; the public baths where, having gone through the turnstile, one still had to wait; the cinema where only three of us would be left at the end; the little square where stood a statue whose unveiling I remembered every time I saw it, because I had been there on the day of the ceremony; the post-office where the door makes a noise which surprises nobody and one can ask for stamps at any of the positions.

Nothing had aged. A hoarding hid an old building which was being demolished. In my absence a trades-man had renovated his shop, a street had been mac-adamised, a café had been enlarged.

Life had gone on. In those who surrounded me I sensed a patient determination to make it more agree-able and that, at the point when I was beginning it again as before, lagging behind them, plunged me into deepest gloom.

I went into a restaurant and sat down near the cash-desk as I always do, as I used to sit near the teacher at school and near the corporal in the army, because I like to feel some source of authority near me. I took off my overcoat. I shook it out before putting it on the chair so that it should lie uncreased. I had my lunch in silence, without appetite, so quickly that as I went out I recog-nized people who had started before me still at table.

The streets were deserted. The sunlight which filled them grew dim without disappearing. The moon, as close to the sun as it could be, was transparent, of a blue so light that one had to search for it before it could be found again.

A street ran straight uphill ahead of me.

I like being high up, with a wide open space before me. I sometimes need to look ahead as far as my eyes can see, to look as far as the point to which the air I breathe extends. My sufferings become less great. Little by little they melt into the sufferings of everyone around me. I no longer suffer alone. To think that, in

110

one of those houses stretching out of sight, there lives a man who perhaps is like me, comforts me. Then the world seems less distant, its joys and sorrows deeper and more of a piece.

I went up the sloping street. Children were playing ball there, the little ones higher up, the big ones lower down, so that their chances were equal.